Danny Appleseed Tinker, Teacher, and Baby Maker

A.G. Kimbrough

Published by A.G. Kimbrough, 2017.

This is a work of fiction. Similarities to real people, places, or events are entirely coincidental.

DANNY APPLESEED TINKER, TEACHER, AND BABY MAKER

First edition. November 1, 2017.

ISBN: 979-8223151241

Written by A.G. Kimbrough.

Table of Contents

Danny Appleseed Tinker, Teacher,

and

Baby Maker

By

A. G. Kimbrough

Copyright © 2017

D2D Edition

All Rights Reserved

Prologue

THE NEW MEXICO PLAINS were burning, and the rains were sparse throughout the crash. The rains stopped completely the same year the drug cartel gangs pushed north and west into the area. The gangs bypassed the few locations where the people mounted a stiff defense, preferring to concentrate on soft and undefended targets. Besides murder, torture, rape and plunder, these desperate men brought the plague.

The plague was created in a secret laboratory, financed by a powerful group with origins in the 1600's. The plague, designed with the single objective of providing a significant population reduction, leaving no long-term threat to the survivors and their rulers. It was delivered from a bunker high in the mountains of South America when one of three men didn't send the abort command before the control computer's fail-safe program timed out. At that moment. explosive charges blew the blast proof doors off the bunker. A cluster of 12 massive helium-filled balloons emerged from the bunker. Suspended below them was a large container.

The balloons continued to rise, and were carried by the jet stream, higher and higher. By the time the winds carried the package around the world and over the mid-Pacific, it entered the stratosphere. A small explosion triggered by an altitude sensor opened a hatch, and 100 micron sized spores fell out in a steady stream.

It took almost three months for the first spores reached ground level over south America. When even one spore was breathed in, the unfortunate person developed a case of the plague. It had a 50 percent mortality rate and was air transmittable by a cough or sneeze from any victim. Within a year, the infection rate in South America was over 90 percent. The last effect was the infertility of 50 percent of its male survivors.

Mike Cullins was a 23-year-old, 200 pound bully and petty thief. He rode two horses into the ground just ahead of a large cartel force. When he saw the Martin Ranch windmill on the edge of the caprock and pushed his exhausted horse through the highway cut into the Pecos River Valley, he was stopped at the base of the cut by a group of armed men in ambush positions.

Cullins joined them in the battle that decimated the cartel force. The defenders were led by Amos Martin, the owner of the Martin Ranch. His son-in-law, Jason, and Amos were both wounded in the battle, and Cullins helped take them back to the ranch. Jason died a lingering death, and Amos slowly recovered.

Cullins saw opportunity there and quickly made himself indispensable. Jason's wife was pregnant, and not interested in him. However, she had a good looking, and naive younger sister.

Within a few months Cullins was the top hand at the ranch and engaged to the younger daughter.

Over the next ten years, the Pecos River dried up, except for a few pockets, and the water in the other "Bottomless Lakes" disappeared. The lakes, were named in the 1850's by cowboys who couldn't find the bottom using weights on their lariats, because of a fast flowing underground river.

After Amos recovered from his wounds he continued traveling around the area providing Tinker services, trading with scattered settlements, and sometimes salvaging when the opportunity arose. The ranch horse herd had been stolen by an early cartel raid and replacements were not available, except at outrageous costs. He was able to buy a young mule that he used to pull his wagon. Losing the

horses didn't handicap the ranch too much, since the remaining stock
came to the lake for water.

On one trip far outside his normal route, Amos came upon a
partially burned home. Scattered bones in front of the adobe house
included one skull with a bullet hole. He looked inside the unburned
section and found a large, battered open gun safe. The roof over the
kitchen had fallen in, but he could see two pots covered by debris.

An hour's work uncovered three pots and two knives. The setting
sun was shining through the open roof, and Amos was just about ready
to stop and make camp for the night. As he turned to carry his finds
back to the wagon, a flash caught his eye. It didn't look to be silver
like the stainless pots, and he thought it might be a copper pot. It was
under a charred beam, and he decided to check it out before leaving
the next morning. It had been a long, largely unfruitful trip, and he was
more than ready to return to the ranch. He missed his four-year-old
Grandson and loved to spend time with him. His oldest daughter
was getting ready to marry her husband's younger brother, and Danny
needed a father.

The next morning, Amos returned to the kitchen, and checked
the reflection and found it was not from a copper pot. It came from
a gold bar, one of 27 identical bars that were hidden in the rafters.
By sundown, he started back toward the ranch with a fortune in gold
overloading the wagon.

Two days later, he arrived at the ranch after sundown and unloaded
his treasure without being seen.

He told his oldest daughter about his find, after swearing her to
secrecy, until after his death. He didn't tell his youngest daughter
because he didn't trust her husband.

By the time Danny turned six, he had a younger brother, and was
often joining Grandpa on his Tinker trips. Mike was facing a serious
rival in his brother-in-law. The people who worked at the ranch were
loyal to Amos, and with their support, his brother-in-law would inherit

the ranch after Amos died. Mike was determined that his own son Jerry would own the ranch after he passed.

One fall day, while Amos and Danny were on a trip, an early morning fire burned Danny's home and killed his family. Although Mike tried to insist otherwise, Danny lived from that day on, with Amos.

When Danny turned 15, Amos reluctantly told his youngest daughter about the treasure, after first extracting a promise not to tell anyone about it.

That same year Mike insisted that Danny pull his own weight around the ranch. Amos compromised, and Danny worked under Mike's direction any time he wasn't on a Tinkers trip with his Grandpa.

When Danny turned 17, his Aunt let it slip to her husband about the treasure Danny would inherit when Amos died.

Tinkers Damn

DANNY MARTIN WAS COLD, tired, and hungry. He had trekked down the dry bed of the Pecos for three days, before he found the carcass of the damn fool mule. The lead rope still tied on its neck. It had broken its right foreleg, and the coyotes had gutted it, probably before it died.

The cabin had a lamp at the window, and he knew grandfather was waiting up for him. The thought returned, "It was all Jerry's fault, but uncle Mike would blame him, again."

"That you Danny?", his grandfather questioned as the door opened.

"Yes, it's me. The damned mule is dead down near the Hagerman ruins. Stepped in a hole and broke a foreleg. Jerry didn't tie the lead rope right, and uncle Mike's gonna blame me. I'm tired of him treat'n me like a slave, while Jerry and his friends can get away with anything."

Danny noticed that the old man had not risen from his bed, with his face drawn and gray. "It looks like you're feeling poorly tonight?"

"Been goin down hill since you left. There's bacon and beans on the stove. Fire it up and while it's heating we need to talk."

Danny rekindled the fire and heated his supper.

"I'm not goin to make it much longer, and there's things you need to know. When I'm gone, your uncle Mike is gonna kill you. He's married to my younger daughter, but you are my oldest daughter's son. That means you will own this homestead and the gold that's hid below the fireplace."

Danny replied, "I'm only 17, surely he wouldn't consider me a threat."

"Your gonna be 18 next week, and the other thing is the Rutherford girl. He wants her for Jerry, and she likes you better. Believe me, the only thing that has protected you so far is me. Leave now to be safe. They don't know you're back, so you can be gone before daylight. I have what you need in a pack under my bed. I wish I could do more, but the cancer has taken all my strength."

"You should follow the riverbed north and on to Fort Sumner. There should be enough water holes and game to see you through. You will be on your own from now on, so be careful and not too trusting."

"My tinkers tools are in the pack. Everybody needs something fixed or sharpened. Should be good for a meal or two on the road. I also put all the cash I have in a leather bag. Put the dimes in your money belt and hide the rest. The gold bars are too heavy to carry, so we'll leave them be. If you ever get back here, you know where to find them."

Danny finished his meal while his grandfather continued to give him advice about making his way in the world.

The old man finished talking when Danny was full and nodding off.

"Now you get a few hours sleep. I'll wake you when it's time to go."

On My Own

IT SEEMED LIKE I HAD just closed my eyes when Gramps shook me awake. He handed me a cup of tea, his pack, and a bacon and bean burrito.

"It's time, Danny. I love you and hope you have a good life. I don't think the rains will come back for a long time. Keep moving till you find a place with plenty of good water. Now git."

I hugged Gramps and said I loved him. Then I shrugged the pack on, finished the tea, and walked away from the community where I had lived all my life.

I remembered the last words I heard from my uncle, "Don't blame Jerry for your fuck up. You're not worth a Tinker's Damn. Now get after the mule, and don't come back without bringing it, or I'll beat you worse than you can imagine."

By the time the sun came over the caprock, I was five miles north and being careful not to leave a trail.

I was carrying a crossbow and a quiver with a dozen quarrels. I made it last spring under Gramps careful guidance. It was sized for me, but it still had a 50 yard killing range and I had used it to bring down a deer.

After making a dry camp at sundown and building a small fire behind a boulder, I doubted Uncle Mike was in pursuit yet, but I didn't want to take a chance of being spotted.

I boiled a handful of parched corn and dried beans in my only pot. While it cooked, I searched the contents of my pack. Besides bags of parched corn, dried beans, and goat jerky, I found fishing line and a tin box full of hooks inside the cook pot. Gramp's tool pouch contained a sewing kit, a skinning knife, a small hammer, a folding multi-tool, a small Crescent wrench, and a set of files. They all were salvaged over his lifetime, and I knew that he treasured them, because he would let no one, not even me, touch them.

A second pouch contained a double handful of silver dimes and five gold eagles. Paper money was worthless, but the pouch represented a small fortune.

My eyes filled with tears when the fact that Gramps was really gone from my life struck home. Sleep that night was troubled even though I had slept alone under the stars many times before. The difference, was that I no longer had a home and family to return to.

I rose with the sun and continued north. At mid day, I filled my canteen at a water hole and noticed a fresh set of antelope tracks leading up a dry wash. I was hungry, and the prospect of fresh meat was appealing.

I lost the trail a half mile up the wash as the sandy wash floor became rock. Realizing I was probably wasting my time, I resolved to turn back if I couldn't pick the trail back up by the time I reached a bend in the wash that was 200 yards away. I reached the bend, with no sign of the tracks. As I turned back toward the river, I noticed a reflection of the afternoon sun. It came from the next bend in the wash and was probably a piece of mica. I continued the turn, and then curiosity overcame my impatience.

I rounded the next bend and found a vehicle hung up on a rock. Most of the vehicles I saw before were stripped years ago. This one was intact. The tires were flat and there were two skeletons in the front seat. I approached, thinking there might be something useful for me to salvage. The door was rusted shut, so I used a rock to break a back window and wiggle inside. I noticed both the passenger, and the driver had small holes in their skulls. They were holding hands. There was an open box of 22 shells on the console, along with an empty holster. A further search revealed a small revolver on the drivers side floor. There were two fired shells in the gun's cylinder.

There were two bicycles on the spare tire rack with flat tires and some rust, but they might be salvageable.

I spent the next two days salvaging the vehicle. There was a lot of stuff I couldn't use, but I found something better than gold. Inside a plastic rooftop carrier was a folding two-wheeled trailer, again with flat tires, but in good shape. It was designed to be pulled from a bracket on the man's bike. Most of the time was spent restoring the man's bike and stripping spare parts off the ladies bike.

I also found a few other items including: a sleeping bag, a little pop up tent, a heavy coat, a pair of good boots that fit, a full five gallon water container, a pair of tire pumps and a bike repair kit. There was a lot of dried and canned food, but since it was so old I didn't want to risk eating it.

When I departed, the filled trailer was connected to the bike and my pack was strapped to the rack over the back wheel. The pistol, holstered on my belt and the crossbow and quiver were strapped across the handlebars.

I had to dismount and push through sand and other rough places, but I still made better time than walking.

Three days later I reached highway 70 at dusk. I came to a conclusion that following the river on the bike was too slow. Taking 70 east wouldn't be good because there was no water on the plains. Taking 70 back toward Roswell would require backtracking a few miles before I could take 285 north. Both 70 and 285 were four lanes and even though the asphalt was cracked and degraded, I could make good time.

I reached 285 before noon the next morning and turned north. That night I camped at the junction with highway 120, the road to Fort Sumner. I studied the map by the light of my campfire and stayed on

285 toward Santa Fe. I had no real reason except I remembered reading somewhere that Santa Fe was the capital of New Mexico back before the crash, and I was curious.

The next morning, on my eighteenth birthday, I continued north on 285. Over the next two days I saw no signs of water and one antelope. Just before sundown I saw a windmill on the horizon ahead. I picked up my pace and a cluster of buildings with some livestock came into view.

There was an exit and a dirt road leading toward the group of buildings, which I took. I suppose it was foolish to approach an unknown homestead at sundown, but I was hungry and lonesome for human contact.

I stopped in front of a building with a lighted window and called. "Hello the house. I'm a Tinker looking to trade fixing and sharpening for a hot meal."

After a long minute the door opened and a man with a long gun stepped out. "Who are you? Step over to the light so I can see better."

I dismounted and approached the door as another man came out holding a lantern. "My name's Danny Martin from down toward Roswell. I have a 22 pistol on my belt, but I mean no harm. I'm gonna take it out slowly and lay it on the step."

By the time I completed the process, the men were joined by two women and two girls that were close to my age.

"He's not gonna cause any harm. This is my husband Claude Esslinger, my daughter Cindy, my sister Betty, her husband Roger Stone, and theirs daughter Millicent. I'm Myrtle. Come on inside and join us for supper."

I spent three days at their ranch, fixing many things and sharpening all their cutlery. With the only water for miles around, they kept around a hundred head of cattle, a string of horses, and two dozen chickens. Every fall they would take half their cattle to Vaughn for sale or trade for the things needed by the ranch. Other than those visits they remained isolated, self contained, and rarely saw visitors.

Cindy was a year younger than me and immature, while Millicent was my age and had developed nicely. I slept in the barn the first night, but the second night, Millicent brought me a blanket, an hour after the lights in the house were out.

She said that she was afraid I might get cold, but I could tell she had something else on her mind. I was in my sleeping bag when she arrived and she spread the blanket over it and sat down beside me.

Millicent was wearing a pink nightgown and said, "I guess it's not very cold now. I'm too warm at the moment. I'll just slip this gown off."

And she did. We got little sleep that night, or the next.

She was crying as I packed up to leave the last morning, and kept asking me to be sure to visit after my business up north was complete. Everyone was nice and told me to hurry back.

As I rode away I had the distinct feeling that there must have been some parental involvement in my nightly visits. She was a nice girl, and I loved the sex. It was even better than with Becky Rutherford. But, I was a long way from being ready to settle down and take on the responsibilities of a family.

Vaughn was a dusty village in the midst of the ruins of a larger town. After topping off my water and buying a couple of things at a store, I dry camped for the night on a hill overlooking the town. I picked that spot so I could see anyone approaching. Having an uneasy the whole time I was there. Several of the guys I saw were a little too interested in my bike and gear. I kept the pistol close as I dropped off to sleep. The next morning I left at dawn and kept an eye on the road behind me all day long. By pushing hard I reached the junction of I 40 by sundown.

There was a freight wagon camped there, and I asked the driver if he minded me joining him. Jake Bidwell was glad for the company and the added security of another man in camp. He was on his way east to

Santa Rosa with a load of grain After a shared meal we talked for a while. I was careful not to say too much and said I was from a ranch south of Vaughn. He gossiped about recent happenings on the Road.

"Oh yea, the other day I ran into a guy headed toward Albq from Roswell. He told me there was a murder there last month. A kid killed his grandfather and stole some stuff and a mule before running away. His uncle was offering a big reward for him dead or alive."

I was sure I turned pale, but Jake kept on talking, this time about the wives he had at each end of his freight run. After a while, I said I was tired and went to bed. I lay awake for some time, thinking about how to avoid the threat from my uncle. I had planned to stop in Santa Fe and stay there through the winter, but that choice did not seem to be safe.

The next morning, I said goodbye to Jake and continued northwest on 285. I took a week to reach Santa Fe, and along the way I avoided other travelers. I took the eastern bypass around Santa Fe. The city was still in ruins, but looked like it still had a population of several hundred.

I stayed east of Santa Fe heading north on State road 590. It took me another week to reach the hamlet of Tesque. There were about a dozen families living there, and since I couldn't avoid being seen, I stopped and played the Tinker's roll. I was welcomed with a hot meal and some information. The town had avoided the plague, since the migration of the cartels had bypassed it. When I mentioned I was looking for a safe place where I could work and spend the winter. They suggested Taos, which was short of manpower. The community lost over half the population in the fights with the cartel and the plague they brought with them.

The next day, I rode through the Indian reservation and the ruins of Espanola and camped in the shell of a burned out school at the junction of Highway 68. Many of the communities had just been abandoned, leaving the buildings to be salvaged for metal, building materials, or firewood. The combinations of first loosing half the population and

then the later infertility of half the men proved too much for many of
the smaller communities.

I was sheltered from the direct effects of the plague, since the
homestead was remote from Roswell, and well enough armed to
prevent the cartel raiders from approaching. The secondary effect,
however, was that my father was killed in the last battle, after
impregnating my mother with me.

The road up to Taos was a tough climb, and it took a day and a half
to reach it.

It was Market Day, and the Plaza was full of people selling and
trading all kinds of things from blankets spread on the sidewalk. I
pushed my bike around looking at everything. When I smelled
something good, I found a Mexican woman selling tacos, and bought
five for a dime. I continued looking around while I ate and they were
delicious. There must have been over 200 people in the plaza, about
half Indians, one quarter Mexican, and one quarter Anglo.

After my first circuit, I found an open spot and spread my blanket
and made a sign that said, "I'm a Tinker and I can fix or sharpen most
anything."

I sat down and spent the rest of the afternoon answering questions,
mostly about my bike and trailer, and sharpening a few knives.

The shadows were crossing the Plaza, and I was thinking about
finding a place to camp for the night, when a well dressed Mexican man
stopped in front of me.

"Good afternoon, sir. I am Francisco Garza. Do you know anything
about steam engines?"

The question surprised me, and I replied, "Yes sir. My grandfather
built a steam powered pump to irrigate the garden, and I helped him
keep it running. It was a fairly simple machine, but I understood how it
worked."

Mr. Garza looked to be in his forties and fit. He looked closely at my bike and the tools I had spread in front of me on the blanket. He smiled and said, "I believe you can help me solve a problem.

"I have a large apple orchard and we make lots of cider. Our main press is powered by a steam engine which has broken. We used the manual presses on last year's crop, but half had spoiled before we could get it all pressed. So far, no one has fixed the steam engine.

"Please come out to my hacienda and look at the steam engine. I'll give you a silver dollar, just to take a look. If you can fix it, I'll make it well worth your time."

"I was looking for a place to work over the winter. I'll be pleased to take a look for a job and a warm place to stay over the winter"

"We can always find a place for someone willing to work, but I insist on giving you an advance on your pay."

He opened a pouch and counted out ten silver dimes. Dropping in my hand he said. "Why don't you pack up your things so we can get back to the hacienda before dark."

Supper, that evening with the Garza family was wonderful. Mrs. Garza was also in her forties, and their five children ranged from teenagers to a toddler. I had a room in the ground floor of the main house, where my stuff and the bike would be safe.

The next day, Sunday, was a day of rest at the Ranch, and Mr. Garza told me to rest from my travels and look around. I ate breakfast in the huge kitchen with most of the household staff and their families. The food was good and although only a few of the adults spoke English, I felt welcome.

During the morning, I explored the area around the Main House. There were three large buildings, a hay and grain storage barn, a livestock barn, and a distillery. Within a half mile were several scattered homes, each with it's own garden plot. An orchard was covering the Western hillside and livestock grazed along the Eastern hills.

I returned for lunch in the Kitchen around noon and then discovered a large library on the second floor that Mr. Garza had suggested I explore. Most of the books were in Spanish, and I resolved to learn to speak and read that language.

Again, I had supper with the family. After breakfast, we rode over to the Press Building. I spent the morning carefully studying the press and the engine supposed to drive it. Mr. Rojas, the press supervisor could not speak English, so Mr. Garza translated. Rojas reported that when they fired it up for the first time last year, steam was escaping from around the connecting rods of both cylinders, and they would not drive the press.

After spending the rest of the morning doing a detailed inspection, I concluded that there must have been water left in the system, which froze and cracked either the pistons or the cylinder blocks.

Around noon, a lunch basket appeared, and I realized I was hungry. Over lunch, I asked about the machine's history. It was built before the plague, by the man who was then the press supervisor. He was killed, along with his assistant, in the last battle with the cartel invaders.

Over the next three days, we worked to disassemble the machine. Progress slowed because I had to make two wrenches to remove the linkages. I found cracks in both the pistons and the cylinder walls.

It was necessary to build a forge to weld up the cracks in the cylinders, and to cast new pistons. That effort took two weeks. During the same two weeks, I built a wood framed lathe powered from a leather belt coupled to an existing water wheel.

The apple crop harvest continued as we raced to complete the repairs. The wooden lathe and tooling was made from salvaged bits and pieces, held together by carved wooden structures, which often broke.

Finally, 45 days after the start, the press was back in operation, just in time to press the harvest. To say that Mr. Garza was pleased was an understatement.

Over the next month, the crop was pressed, with the engine running 20 hours a day. I spent most of every day at the press and was on call any time I was not.

On the first Market Day after the crop was pressed, I returned to the Plaza. I had read all the English books in the Garza library and remembered seeing a few at one booth. Although I was not looking for work since I had a good job and plenty of money, I was eager to spend time with an English speaking female.

When I found the booth in front of a two story adobe home, there was a good-looking young woman there. She was nice, but made it clear she wasn't interested in my attempts to start a conversation. After looking carefully at the small groups of books, I concluded there wasn't anything I was interested in. Most were catalogs from before the crash, or either romance novels, or books I had already read.

Turning to her, I remarked, "Are these the only books you have?"

"Goodness no, we aren't illiterate, father had a huge library, but we won't consider selling any of those books."

"Well, I won't be buying any of this crap. Could I look at your library, please?"

"You're a rude young man. There is no way I'll even let you set a foot in our home, much less look at father's library."

I was getting ready to walk away, when a voice from behind me spoke out.

"Beth you're the one being rude. Just because you don't like men is no excuse. Please come in with me, sir. We are proud of our father's library."

The voice belonged to Beth's older sister Mikea Carter. Their father was a teacher, before the last battle, where he was killed.

The upper floor of their storefront was where the sisters lived. The stairway came into a large room, with every wall covered in bookshelves. I was mesmerized by more books than I had seen in my lifetime. With my mouth hanging open, I walked along the shelves in amazement. There were many books I had to read.

"I know that none of these books are for sale, but would you let me rent a few, just long enough to read them. Look, I'll give you a silver dollar to hold as security, and a silver dime to rent all the books I can read in a month. I'll come to your shop every Market Day and exchange the ones I have read for different ones."

Mikea though about my offer for a while. She knew that I was working for Mr. Garza, and figured he would be sure to make me return the books. She knew the silver dollar was a lot of money, and the dime rent was generous.

I was ecstatic when she agreed to my offer, and almost gave her a hug. But, she flinched when I approached. I stopped, smiled, and held out my hand which, she accepted with a brief smile of relief.

Over the late fall and winter I devoured at least five books every week. I also developed a tenuous friendship with the sisters. I learned that both were raped in the same attack, when their father was killed. They wanted nothing to do with any man and had spurned many suitors over the years. They also were open about their lesbian relationship.

The last storm of winter had included a hard freeze. The following Market Day I returned another stack of books, and Mikea asked me to look at a problem with their water system. They had an inside hand pump on their shallow well which forced water into a tank on the roof. That tank fed the cold water pipes in the bathroom and the kitchen and had an overflow into a large black plastic tank that fed the solar heated hot water for the shower. The hot water tank had an overflow outlet that drained into the kitchen sink.

The freeze cracked a fitting on the roof and drained the main cold water tank.

I spent the afternoon finding the replacement fittings. I returned to pick up my books and promised Mikea to return the following day and make the repairs.

After breakfast, I gathered my tools and found a beautiful day. The sun was shining brightly, and there was no breeze. It took until the early afternoon to complete the repairs on the roof, and it was hot. I was drenched with sweat when I came into the kitchen to pump water back into the tank.

Since I sunburn easily, I left my shirt on while working on the roof. I took it off before I started pumping because the kitchen stove was hot with something in the oven. The kitchen was even warmer than the roof had been.

It took 45 minutes to fill the tank, and I was bushed, and still drenched in sweat. I asked Beth to watch the fittings on the roof for leaks as I filled the tank and she reported that there were none.

Mikea had been watching my efforts in the kitchen and said, "I'm roasting a chicken for your supper, but I suppose it wasn't such a good idea. Why don't you take a shower upstairs before supper"

I was sure I was smelling like a horse and sweating like one. "That's a good idea, if you don't mind."

"Sure go right ahead."

I walked upstairs and rinsed out and hung my shirt to dry first, because it was stinky too. The bathroom was off the bedroom and I had closed the door as I entered. I took off my pants and turned to adjust the shower.

I heard the click of the door opening and turned to see both Beth and Mikea standing there, stark naked.

Mikea said, "we decided that a shower would be good. You don't mind if we join you?"

I think my face was turning red, but I stammered out, "You can, the water's just right. But, but I thought you don't like men."

The shower was large, and I backed toward the far wall, with my hand attempting to cover the obvious developing erection. Mikea was nearest, and she put a hand on my chest.

"We don't, but you're an exception. You're a friend and a decent man, and we need something. We want children, and would like to have you try to provide them."

"You mean, have sex with you?"

"That's the way it's normally done, isn't it?" She said, as she grasped my erect member.

"But you're lesbians."

My comment was interrupted when Beth hugged me from behind, pressing her naked body against me, as she said. "I guess we will have to become bi-sexual in your case."

The shower was delightful, uninhibited, and memorable. We spent the afternoon in their bed and only left it when the chicken was in danger of burning. It was an experience where I learned a lot, especially about a women's pleasure centers. I could tell that they were not too comfortable with male/female sex, but they were trying hard to organism with me. Afterward, I found their mutually generated organisms excited me, and I was soon ready to return to the field.

During our nude supper, they made it clear I would be under no obligation for the child or children that may result from this, or future lovemaking. Neither wanted a man in their, or their children's lives. I readily agreed since my long-term plans were to move on, eventually.

I returned to my place at the Garza ranch after a final round of lovemaking, and I took two days to recover. The visits continued regularly until both ladies had missed their periods.

I've found that ladies talk much more freely about some subjects than men. Shortly after my trysts with the Carter sisters were completed, I had a knock on my door one evening. I had moved to a room off the plaza to service my developing tinker's business, to teach reading classes, and to be closer to the Carter sisters.

My visitor was Harlan Sims, who ran a salvaged printing press to make handbills and other small print jobs.

"Mr. Martin, my wife and I would like you to join us for supper tomorrow night. We want to discuss the thing you helped the Carter sisters with."

He was agitated, and red in the face, so I agreed to meet them a half hour after sundown the next night.

I had looked around for a lady friend after the Carter sisters, but all the possible subjects made it clear they were looking for a husband, and a lifelong commitment. That was something where I had absolutely no interest. I was still working two or three days a week at the Garza ranch, teaching his kids and fixing a few things, but I could see I would probably move on next spring.

The door was answered by Mrs. Sims. "Thanks for coming over Mr. Martin."

"Please call me Danny."

"Fine, if you'll call me Sally."

Sally was a trim brunette in her late 20's or early 30's.

She led me into her kitchen where Harlan poured wine and Sally served our supper. The conservation was light during the meal, with Sally doing most of the talking.

After the dishes were cleared and the apple brandy poured, Sally started the serious conversation.

"We're desperate to have a child, and Harlan appears to be infertile. His father survived the plague, but. We would like for you to give us the same service you provided to the Carter sisters. We"ve talked about it and believe this is the best chance for us to have a child to love."

I looked across the table at Harlan, who was again, flushed. "Are you sure this is something you are sure of?"

He answered without hesitation, "Oh, I'm sure. It's embarrassing, but having a child for us to love is the most important thing. We would like it not to become common knowledge, but I'm confident enough in our love to not be jealous."

"I will be most discreet. I can't make any guarantees, but I'll do my best. Sally, we should make love every two or three days around the center of your menstrual cycle. I can come over after dark and leave before dawn. Harlan, we would all be more comfortable if you weren't here when Sally and I are making love."

Sally was also blushing, but she responded, "Great, I believe tonight is a good time to start. Harlan darling, you can take your blankets down to the shop. I'll have a good breakfast ready in the morning."

They kissed, and he picked up his blankets and went downstairs.

Sally turned with tears in her eyes and said, "That was the hardest thing I've ever done. No man has ever seen me naked, or touched me there, except Harlan. I almost feel like I'm gonna betray him."

I rose from the table and answered, "We don't have to go through with this if you don't feel right."

"No, I feel a little guilty, because I'm a little excited by the thought of it. Come on into the bedroom before I get cold feet. I want this baby more than anything in my life."

I followed her into the bedroom and waited while she lit the lamp. She looked over her shoulder and asked me to unbutton the back of her dress. It fell to the floor, and she was naked. She hesitated for a moment and turned around.

"Now it's your turn Danny"

I stared at her while I slowly unbuttoned my shirt. She was flushed, and both nipples were erect. I stepped out of my shoes, unbuckled my belt, and let my pants fall. I was fully erect.

"Like what you see?" I asked

"I surely do. Now take me to bed, it's getting cold in here."

She trembled when I took her in my arms, but gave me a deep kiss as I carried her to the bed.

I laid her on her back, leaned over, and kissed both nipples. Holding them, I said, "These breasts are longing to suckle your child."

She shuddered, "Yes."

I ran my right hand up from her knee to the junction of her thighs, and she shuddered again. Her fingers found my cock and squeezed it.

"Come on up here and give me what I need. You're not fuckin a virgin."

I straddled her knees and gave her a deep kiss after spreading her lips. She tasted sweet and shuddered again as I repeated the kiss.

"You're no virgin either. So please fuck me before I come. I want that cock deep inside me now."

I was exited, and hard as a rock. I was able to enter her slowly and deliberately, but her thrusts soon overcame my best efforts of control. My organism was massive, and I didn't withdraw. After 30 seconds of savoring the moment, she shuddered and had one of her own that, left us both gasping.

She breathlessly remarked, "That was wonderful, you curled my toes that time."

"Much obliged, my lady."

Our second time was slower paced. She woke me for a quick one before dawn, and that was still good. I left, feeling pleased with myself, when the eastern horizon was just turning color. If Harlan was awake when I crept by him, he said nothing.

Our liaisons continued until she missed her period. By then, I had three other "clients", and I was booked completely. I was having a busy life, with working for Mr. Garza three days a week, and teaching four different classes to a mixture of students. I still played Tinker when called upon and spent every Market Day morning reading stories to a growing group of younger kids in the Plaza.

Pleased with my new life and my new calling, I was reconsidering my decision to leave in the Spring. Now well known here and liked in the Mexican and Anglo communities, I even had several friends in the Indian community.

However, that chapter in my life came to an end on a Market Day in late fall.

A New Beginning

THE DAY STARTED NORMALLY, with a quick breakfast at Maria's cafe. The market vendors were getting set up when I retrieved my rocking chair, placed it in a sunny spot, and pulled out the copy of Treasure Island. I read part of it to the kids last week, and there were a dozen of them waiting as I set my chair down. Most of them were children of the vendors, whose patients were glad to have them occupied while they were setting up their stalls.

At high noon, I stopped reading, put away my rocking chair and book, and retrieved a shopping bag.

I always checked out all the vendors, because their wares often changed depending on what was harvested, or crafted, or salvaged, or traded. Although I was on the lookout for tools, books, or bike parts, the only thing I bought that afternoon was a tattered 2014 farmer's almanac, some fresh vegetables, and a side of bacon.

Because I wasn't expecting to make a major buy, I only had a few dimes in my money belt, and didn't need to access the hidden bag with the rest of my still sizable stash of silver and gold coins. I always was careful to be frugal and live with the money I earned.

Supper was scheduled with my newest clients, the Anderson's, who I would meet after sundown. I didn't know where they lived, so Mr. Anderson would come by my place to take me to his home.

I was eager to study the almanac since the last one I read had useful bits of information I could use. When I unlocked the door to my room, a voice behind me interrupted.

"Danny Martin!"

When I turned to face a large man who grabbed my shoulder and finished spinning me around. "Yea, what the hell?"

He shoved me backward into and through the door.

"That's him all right." shouted a second man.

I started to recover from my backward stumble when something hit me hard.

The first thing I noticed was the pain in my jaw and the blood in my mouth. My vision was clouded, and I was tied to a chair. I heard a crash and looked to see my bike and trailer falling to the floor from the rafters. The larger guy picked up the trailer and dumped the basket contents on the floor.

Both men were ransacking my place, looking for something. I noticed that my money belt was gone.

The smaller man with a face like a weasel, slapped me, and my nose bled.

"Where is your stash? The poster said you stole a mule and the old man's gold."

"I don't know what you're talking about. All I have is in my money belt, and you already stole that."

"We confiscated it, for expenses. We're entitled to that since we're authorized Bounty Hunters, and we got the poster to prove it."

About that time Mr. Anderson knocked on the open door.

"What in the hell are you doing?" He demanded, as he pushed into the room.

He then noticed that both men were armed. I started to say something, but the smaller man slapped me and I saw stars again.

My ears were ringing from the blows, but I dimly heard the response.

"We have apprehended the fugitive Danny Martin, who is wanted by the Roswell sheriff for the murder of his own grandfather and the theft of a mule and other valuables. We are authorized Bounty Hunters, and this young man is worth 500 silver dollars, Dead or Alive If you interfere, we can shoot you down like a dog. Now get!"

Mr. Anderson was not a coward, but he wasn't a fool either. My vision cleared just as he backed out of the room.

The large man spoke. "We better just shoot him and get the hell out of here."

"I don't want to smell his stinking corpse all the way back to Roswell. When we get away from here we can encourage him to tell us where the stash is hidden. Now go get the horses."

A few minutes later I was tied across a pack-horse leaving Taos. I must have passed out, because the next thing I remember is the big guy dumping me on the ground, and dragging me over to a tree. He tied me to it, and I noticed that it was pitch dark. The two guys made a rough camp and sat around a fire for a couple of hours before I dozed.

Later, I woke, cold, thirsty, and hungry. It must have been near dawn because the sky in the east was becoming lighter. The small guy was sleeping and the large guy was sitting by the fire with his back to me. I tried, but my bonds seemed even tighter than before, and I had no feeling in my hands.

I knew my uncle wanted me dead, and his power as the primary source of water in the area would make any trial a farce. These two Bounty Hunters were taking no chances of me escaping, and would kill me if I tried anything.

Suddenly, I felt my bonds loosen. My hands were too numb, but I felt the ropes loosen on my arms. I remained frozen in position, afraid that the big guy might notice something.

I caught a flicker of motion to my right, and a lariat fell around the seated man's shoulders.

"What the hell?" he exclaimed as he rose, struggling to free the rope.

At the noise, the smaller guy threw his blanket off and reached for his gun. He stopped as a rifle barrel appeared in front of his face.

The lariat tightened and jerked the large guy to the ground. Within seconds four masked and armed men appeared, and both Bounty Hunters were hogtied, disarmed, and bootless.

One of the masked men, who sounded a lot like Mr. Sims, said. "We'll be taking your boots, horses, and gear as compensation for the damage you caused in Taos. This better be your last lesson. If you come back, you will be hung. You should be able to get out of those ropes in a little while. When you do, you better get walking toward Santa Fe, cause there's a storm brewing."

I was helped to my feet and mounted by a masked man who turned out to be Mr. Anderson. My other rescuers were former and current clients.

We reached Taos by mid afternoon, and I was in rough shape. I had lost one tooth with two others loosened, and Mr. Anderson said I probably had a concussion. He insisted on taking me to his house to recover.

I spent the next week recuperating under the care of Mrs. Anderson, who kept me in bed, naked, and often not alone. I had just returned to my place, where I found everything restored, when Mr. Garza visited me.

"It's good to see you up and around Danny."

I replied, "I should be able to come back to work in a couple more days."

"That won't be necessary. You're no longer safe here, my friend. It's likely that those Bounty Hunters will return with a posse. We could fight them off, but I know you wouldn't want to see any of your friends hurt or killed."

"No, I surely don't want that. I'll get packed up and be gone right away." I replied.

"I think you should take another week to finish healing. I have an idea about a safe place for you to spend the winter, but it will take a few days to confirm it."

I spent the next week visiting my clients. I gave them each an apple seed and asked them to plant it in their garden after their child arrived. I told them that as the seed and their child grew, the tree would be a reminder of the young man who helped them start a family.

I was packed up and ready to go by the next Market Day when Mr. Garza returned.

He was smiling, and I felt relieved.

"I sent my oldest son Ramon to the town of Red River. We have traded with that community for years and I believe it will be a safe place for you to winter, since it's remote, and will soon be snowed in until late Spring."

Red River

MR. GARZA GAVE ME A brief rundown on the town of Red River. "It was a mining center from the late 1800's until the 1950's, when the mines closed. A ski resort was built in 1990, and it operated until the crash.

"As the crash developed, a group of five wealthy families bought the entire town, the ski resort, and all the surrounding properties. They built a huge self sustaining refuge for a few friends and families. The head of each family took a blood oath with the heads of the other four families and pledged a bond of mutual support.

"The families and their mutual bonds exist today. The plague reached Red River, with the same results we in Taos experienced. We are trading partners after the winter months, when we sell mostly beef, grains, cider, and wool. They trade gold, silver, gunpowder, flintlock firearms, and other machined items.

"They have maintained two small hydro-electric power stations and a large solar system all these years, and use it to provide power for lighting, heating, and some manufacturing. Most of the people live inside a huge structure that has the upper floors configured as a greenhouse. During the last part of the crash years the town was closed to outsiders, and two different large groups of cartel invaders were wiped out when they tried to attack the town. They opened the town for trade about 15 years ago and have been a good neighbor.

"The elected head of the families is David Franklin. He is the man who authorized your visit. He is also the head of one of the families."

It took two days to make it to the community of Red River. Mr. Garza suggested I take the back way since there would be less opportunity to be seen and possibly reported if a posse should come that way. The only community I needed to pass was the small town of Eagle Nest. I camped five miles before it, rode through just before dawn, and reached Red River late the same day. On the road at the east end of town I found a manned guard house.

I stopped, and explained who I was, and that Mr. Franklin was expecting me. The guard told me to wait while he called city hall. I knew about the telephone systems and had seen pieces of equipment. But I had never heard of it working in our day and age. He turned a crank and then spoke into a microphone while he listened to a headset.

After a minute, he came out and told me to ride into town, turn right, and go up the hill to the big glass building. I followed East Main Street for five minutes and turned toward the largest building I ever saw. The road ended at a pair of metal doors on the ground level. There was a guard station beside a small door, and one of the big doors opened as I approached. I rode inside and found a ramp leading down to a large room. I stopped at the entrance and the guard asked if I was Danny Martin. When I answered in the affirmative, he told me to ride down to the parking area, park, and wait for my escort.

Five minutes later I was joining David Franklin and his family, for supper at a small restaurant on the ground floor. The view above us was open through the multiple levels of the gardens to the glass roof, and the stars were spectacular. The families welcome was warm, and I mentally thanked Mr. Garza for what must have been a stellar introduction. After supper, Rick Franklin, David's oldest Grandson took me to an apartment on the first basement level that would be my winter home. He was my age, and we were friends by the time he helped me bring in my bike and trailer.

The apartment was small and without a kitchen. Rick explained that it was a rental for visitors and temporary employees. My rent would be a silver dollar a month. He said that I would take most of my meals at any of the nearby restaurants on the mall. Rick then said he would be by in the morning to show me around. I was beat from the trip and slept like a log that night.

The next morning I joined Rick and paid two cents for a plain breakfast of oatmeal with fresh blackberries and a cup of real coffee.

Over a second cup, Rick explained that the refuge was built over a two-year period, by the families and their contractors, at a cost of over sixty million dollars. Up close, the building was immense, five thousand feet long, with the glass walls extending up for ninety feet, at a forty-five-degree angle.

Looking up, I saw that the opposite wall was mirrored and reflected the sunlight into the multi-storied, subterranean growing chamber. The plants were growing in containers in tiers to catch the most of either direct or reflected sunlight. I noticed that water was dripping down from the higher containers into the lower ones, and finally into lower level tanks, where the surface was covered with a floating green layer.

Rick explained, "This ecosystem, called aquaponics, provides the ability to grow a wide verity of plants, with no need for chemical fertilizers or large amounts of water. It also provides a continuing supply of fish protein. The fish waste from the lower fish tanks is high in nitrates and ammonia, nutrients necessary for the plants to flourish. It is pumped into the upper growing containers where it feeds the plants and is filtered by the growing media before being returned to the fish tanks.

"We also have chickens running loose on the walkways that keep the bugs under control and gives a steady stream of eggs and meat. The windows are double, separated by a four inch air gap and the inner glass is a transparent solar panel. The electricity they generate provides the power for pumps, heaters and lighting.

"Each of the families has specialized talents and responsibilities. Ours is agriculture. All the families respond to requests for general labor support, such as harvests, snow clearance, and security.

"The Bradly Families specialization is animal husbandry, slaughter and distribution. Several of the basement levels are devoted to animal pens. The animal and harvest waste is collected and applied to a combination of indoor and outdoor composting areas.

"The Weston Family are geologists, civil engineers, and miners. They give facility and infrastructure support and maintenance. They also operate and develop our mineral acquisition processes, including gold mining and smelting operations.

"The Eaton Family provides the maintenance and support for the electric power systems from two different hydro-electric systems, the solar systems, and the water distribution system.

"The Macon Family is our manufacturing group. They have a complete metal working facility that produces limited quantities of items that are not available through trade or salvage. Their most important trade items are flintlock rifles, black powder, and reloading services.

"Together, the Families have provided this community the ability to survive through the crash and the plagues, although we have suffered heavily in the last one. Our families are bound by the original blood oath, and marriages between the families."

My tour continued after lunch, and I was amazed at the level of knowledge and technology that went into the original design, how much had been retained, and was still working over the years. Things were more labor intensive than before the crash, but no one was hungry, and the community wasn't living off of salvaging the pre-crash ruins.

That night, I had supper with Rick and his wife Laura. She was not from any of the families. Her Anglo/Hispanic parents fled Cimarron during the plague. They lived in a home on ground level. Her mother lived with them, and the fact that there were no children was obvious.

The baked trout, with potatoes and fresh vegetables was good. After desert, Laura's mother excused herself, and we enjoyed some more coffee. Rick opened the discussion.

"The letter from Mr. Garza spoke highly of you. It mentioned that you were very helpful to some families that couldn't have a child. I wonder if you will offer that kind of aid while you are here?"

I had been expecting that kind of question as the evening wore on, but wasn't sure how to answer. "I don't know if you understand the type of help I can offer. I would hate to cause an insult, or a misunderstanding."

When I hesitated, Laura said, "Please go on, we're adults here, and at the point where we are desperate to have a child."

I swallowed and replied. "What I can offer, is to attempt to get you pregnant, by making love every two or three days during the days when you are fertile. I can't guarantee success, but I have been in the past."

Rick flushed, and asked. "How often were you successful in Taos?"

"Eight couples that I know of. The last two I don't know about."

"How many did you try?"

"Ten altogether."

Laura started crying, and Rick said, "Can you give us a minute?"

I stood, headed for the door and said, "I hope I didn't offend. I'll be right outside."

I wondered if I had made a huge false step. Ten minutes later, Rick opened the door and asked me in.

Laura still had tears in her eyes. She approached me, put her arms around me, and said. "You can't imagine how happy you have made me. I had despaired of ever being able to have a child of my own."

I looked at Rick, who now had tears, and asked, "Do you feel the same way?"

"Of course I do. We now have hope when before we had none."

We concluded with a discussion on logistics. Laura told me her mother was already a co-conspirator, since she was equally desperate to have a grandchild. Grandma would retire to her room for the night, and Rick would sleep in his office on the nights when I was visiting.

At that point I was expecting to say good night, when Laura said, "Now that is settled, is it too soon to get started?"

I looked at her, and then Rick. "If you're both sure, then I'm okay with beginning tonight."

Rick smiled and said, "I know you're leaving in the Spring, so time is limited and there's no reason to delay."

He stood, kissed his wife, said good night, and left the room.

Laura stood, held out her hand, and I took it.

"This way." She said, and I followed her into their bedroom.

The room had a nice sized bed and a large, floor to ceiling window. She opened the blinds, turned out the lights, and said, "I would like you to undress me in the moonlight."

I embraced her, we kissed, and I started slowly unbuttoning her dress. Her bare skin was chalky white in the moonlight. Another kiss, deeper and longer, and I slipped it off her shoulders to fall on the floor. I stepped back and admired her uncovered body in the moonlight as I slowly undressed.

When my pants hit the floor, she stepped forward, and said. "I thought you would be in a hurry, but I'm glad you're taking your time."

"I'm tempted, but this is more than just raw sex. I believe making love must be intimate, an expression of love, and the first time shouldn't be rushed. We humans have an infinite capacity for love, and my relationship with both of you must include that love and mutual trust. Sex can and should be fun and playful, but this first time you give yourself completely to me is special."

Laura blinked away a tear. "Yes, I can feel this is a special time, and the love you're showing both of us."

She took my hand and lead me to her bed.

Our lovemaking was gentle and slowly increased to a crescendo. We fell asleep entwined and awoke as dawn was breaking. Our second session was more playful and to the point. Afterward, we dressed and joined Rick for a cup of coffee.

The winter passed quickly. I spent my days exploring the huge complex, soaking up information on any subject that could be useful to others, without the technology base.

I visited the weapons shop and traded the 9mm Glock and the 22 pistol for 200 rounds of 45 caliber ammunition for the Ruger. One box of ammunition was modern smokeless powder, and the other was a reload using black powder, which was the only thing available in the world of today. The trade also included a box of 2000 primers, a keg of black powder, a bullet mold, a simple press, and a cleaning kit.

I traded, and bought several different seed packets, which would prove to be valuable trade items.

I also continued my fertility consulting, and as Spring approached, had two confirmed pregnancies, and ten client families. As before in Taos, I visited each family before I departed and gave them an apple seed.

The night before I left, I had supper with Rick and Sally. Afterward, she insisted on stripping down to show me her growing belly in the moonlight. I was eager to depart, but it felt like I was leaving my family. I had never asked for compensation for my services. But I guess the communities capitalistic practices prevailed because each husband pressed a twenty dollar gold eagle in my hand. I would be leaving Red River much more wealthy.

My most recent client was waiting at my door when I returned from the Franklin's. I was ready for sleep but Dianna Parker was insistent and wearing nothing under her robe. Inside my room, I guided her to bed, and she had her way with me before we slept, and a final time the next morning.

There was a group of friends and clients waiting at the doors as I wheeled my bike toward them. After hugs all around I climbed on my bike and headed west on Highway 38.

I made it to the ruins of Questa and camped for the first night. It was still near freezing by morning, and it was good to get back on the road headed north on Highway 522. The only people I saw that day was an Indian family living in an adobe storefront in the ruins of Castila. I gave them a dime for some tamales and continued north.

I camped that night at the state line and continued north on Colorado 159. The country was mostly flat, with visible snow still on the mountains.

I spent time in Red River studying my maps and those I found in the Family library. I decided to head for northern California, where it looked as if it should have a plentiful water supply on the western slopes of the coastal mountains. It also should be far enough to avoid my uncle's bounty hunters. I planned to continue north until I hit US 50 and then follow it all the way to California.

I followed 159 to US160 and turned west. The country was mostly high desert, with occasional abandoned cultivated areas. One tire on the trailer had developed a crack that was getting worse. I had spare tires and tubes for the bike, but not for the trailer. If I couldn't find a replacement tire in Alamosa, I would have a serious problem. The tire split just east of Alamosa, and I jury-rigged a leather wear patch and a wire around the tire to hold it closed.

I found Alamosa to be abandoned, except for a dozen families. The college there shut down after the crash and the students and most of the faculty left. The harsh weather and the worsening drought drove all but a few away. I paid one family for a couple of simple meals and some local information. The oldest, remembered an old man who salvaged several things from the Walmart. He operated a salvage store out of his home for a few years until he died in the plague.

I asked where the house was, even though it had probably been salvaged, and one of the younger family members offered to show it to me in the morning.

Later, I asked about the cartel attacks, since I had seen no burned-out buildings that were their typical signature. The old man told me that the cartel never came through Alamosa. He guessed that was because the town was so far off the main highways. He said that I was the first visitor to come there since everyone left at the end of the crash.

I then questioned, "How did the plague arrive?"

He said he didn't know. Everyone became sick within a two-week period. Those who survived, recovered within a month. Only a few children were born starting a year after the plague. He thinks most of the men are now infertile.

That the plague might not have been spread only by the cartel invaders was becoming a possibility in my mind.

The next day, I searched the abandoned home and garage. The home had been the primary storefront, and it had been well picked over. I found nothing useful The roof of the garage was partially collapsed, but I found a few bikes in the back corner. None of them had what I needed. I dug through the rubble in the collapsed area and found a rack of bike parts, including tires. It took all afternoon to dig them out, but I ended up with two tires, several tube patch kits, and spare tubes for the bike and trailer. I also uncovered a usable mountain bike that I gave to the young man who had shown me the house and helped with the search.

I left the next day and headed northwest on US160/285 to Monte Vista, where I turned north on US285. Monte Vista had been a farming and railroad town, but it looked abandoned. I saw no one as I rode through in midday. The area north had the remains of many crop circles on both sides of the road. It reminded me on similar areas around Roswell, abandoned after either water or power were no longer available to drive the irrigation systems.

I camped overlooking a large abandoned farm complex with rows of low structures that must have been barns.

Over the next two days I passed through a couple of abandoned towns and finally reached the junction of US285 and US50. The town of Pancha Springs was located there, and I was shocked to see a freshly painted sign advertising the Pancha Springs Inn and Restaurant. More than ready for a bed and a meal, I followed the sign to a large single story building.

I found the establishment to be run by a large polygamist family group headed by an obviously fertile man named Brian Sibley. There was at least a dozen children studying under the direction of two women in the lobby. Mr. Sibley checked me in, showed me to my room and told me to join him in the bar for a drink before dinner.

I parked my bike in the room and returned to the lobby.

Sibley got up and led me into the bar. "Please come in. We don't get many travelers this early in the year, and I'm yearning to speak to another man."

"There's not another man living in this town?" I questioned.

"It's a bit of a long story. I'll pour us a beer while I'll try to explain. I sold my BMW dealership in Denver early in the crash after my wife left me for a football star. I left there and bought this place, looking for a refuge from the crash. After the plague played out I met a local Mormon widow. We fell in love, married, and she became pregnant. I was shocked because I assumed, like every man I knew, that I was infertile.

"Six months into her term she brought over a friend who had dumped her asshole husband. The friend told me she might have stayed, but she wanted a child, and her husband proved to be infertile. My wife then asked me to marry her friend and give her a child. I thought it over and agreed.

"A year after my son was born, I had eight wives, and damn near every woman left in town who wanted a child, wanting to be my wife. I was very unpopular with the men in town, and all of them eventually left. I now have 27 wives, and although I love them all, its impossible for me to give them the attention they deserve. We all live here in the inn, and we have unconventional lives. When we have guests here, my wives are welcome to join them if they wish. Must of the men are infertile, but it gives my wives an option to enjoy more than I can supply.

"We have a large soaking tub, where nudity is the rule, and several of my ladies will be there after dinner every evening. I hope you will join us tonight."

I was surprised by this unusual relationship, but replied. "I'll be pleased to, and suggest that any of your ladies are in their fertile window, to be there, since I may be able to leave something behind for them to love."

"That's delightful news. I hope you are planning to stay for a while. I need to consider the marriage prospects for my children and you can help them improve. I have to oversee the meal preparations so I'll leave you to enjoy another mug of beer and see you at seven."

I finished the beer, and returned to my room. After cleaning up, I took a short nap and returned to the lobby for dinner.

I was surprised to find only six women at the table. They were all under 30, good looking, and dressed simply.

Brian was seated at one end of the table and motioned to the last seat at the opposite end. "I see you are looking confused. These ladies meet your requirements, and I kept the group small and intimate."

While we were being served by some other good-looking women, each of the seated ladies introduced herself, and we got acquainted.

The meal was delicious, but not too filling. After desert, the ladies retired and Brian suggested we enjoy a cigar in the library. They returned about the time we were finished, wearing terrycloth robes. We all then retired to the spa, where a large wooden tub filled with steaming hot water awaited. The ladies took off their robes while we both undressed. An hour later, the lady of my choice and I returned to my room to complete the evening.

She woke me early in the morning, and we didn't leave the bed until mid-morning.

I stayed a week with the lovely Sibley ladies, and left with many of those I hadn't had time, or energy for, asking me to please hurry back. I gave those I had enjoyed an apple seed and asked them to plant it if our lovemaking bore fruit.

I also planted disinformation by relating how I was on my way to Denver to meet a friend and then join him in a trek to Chicago.

I had been riding west on US 50 for two and a half days when the weather turned nasty. A cloud bank swept out of the north, pushed by a stiff wind and a freezing rain that came down in a torrent. I was in a mostly flat area and there was no obvious shelter in sight. I decided to climb the rise ahead and if there was no shelter in sight, to just pitch my tent beside the road.

By the time I reached the hilltop, I was soaked. Fortunately I saw a couple of buildings two miles down the road.

By the time I reached them my face and hands were turning blue and I was shivering uncontrollably. With the last of my strength I called for help. I attempted to dismount, but collapsed instead.

I vaguely knew of being helped inside, and a voice saying. "Help me get his wet clothes off, and wrapped up in the blue quilt."

"Stoke the fire up so I can boil some water, and where did you put that bottle of rum?"

I opened my eyes to see a pretty young woman attempting to get me to drink something.

"Drink this, it will warm your insides."

And it did. I noticed there was a man beside her, and they were both wrapped up in blankets.

He said, "I never saw it rain that hard, or be that cold. We both got soaked, just getting you and your stuff inside."

I learned that the couple were John and Hilda Thomas. We spent the rest of the afternoon talking and drinking hot buttered rums. John had stoked up the stove and Hilda hung our wet clothes near it. The sunlight was fading when Hilda started to fix a simple meal. The cabin had warmed up, and she was struggling to keep the blanket up when it slipped off entirely.

John was lighting a lantern at the table, and laughed at her struggle to retrieve and re-position it. "Oh hell Hilda, we saw everything Danny had to show. It's only fair he gets a chance to see ours, though I doubt he's very interested in me."

With a look of defiance she threw her blanket at him and turned to face me. "Well Danny, I guess we'll have a chance to get real acquainted during your visit. Maybe even intimately, just to spice up our sex life. From what I saw, I think you could be up for it."

We were all more than a little drunk, and John replied, "Woman, you're sassy enough tonight, and you're gonna get fucked real good by both of us, starting right now."

He threw his blanket toward the bed and said. "Take that pot off the stove and come here woman."

He turned to me and said, "Are you up for a fuckin good time Danny"?

I was feeling no pain, and ready, but I replied, "I'm ready, but I might make her pregnant. I've done it several times before."

Hilda turned to me and I could see tears in her eyes. "That would be the most wonderful thing that could happen to us."

John injected, "We had given up hope. Please do your best to help us start a family."

I ended up spending a week with the Thomas family. It was weird making love with Hilda with John on the other side of the bed, but it increased all of our excitement levels. After I was spent, she would turn over and take him on.

It took me another three days to reach Gunnison, where I spent a day, buying a few supplies. The days were growing warmer, and the weather improved. After the long winter, I was anxious to keep moving.

Caravan

IT TOOK ANOTHER WEEK of hard riding to reach Grand Junction. As I approached, I saw a double line of tractor trailers pulling into a large open area. I had never seen an internal combustion vehicle in operation and here were 24 of them. There were two tanker trailers and 20 double trailers, which all had windows.

There was a large crowd of local people on horseback and buggys following the caravan, and I joined them.

I spent the afternoon walking around, talking to both locals and some of the caravan inhabitants. I learned that the group had leased the abandoned field to grow a crop of hemp. They used pressed hemp seed oil to power their trucks and planned to spend the summer growing and harvesting their crop.

I camped that night beside one truck after asking permission from the head of one family. Martin Tucker invited me to join his family for supper that night. He and his wife Sara, lived in one half of the 40-foot trailer overlooking my tent. The side of the trailer folded down to form a deck. A folding table completed the outdoor dining room. I insisted on bringing a bottle of hard apple cider, which we enjoyed together.

They explained that they were farmers in the mid-west before the crash and had grown hemp as the availability of diesel went away. Growing hemp was still against the law, but enforcement was non-existent by then. As the growing season became shorter and shorter, the markets for their crops and livestock became unworkable, and the flow of desperate people fleeing the cities looked like it would become a flood. The Tuckers and some of their friends and neighbors thought about alternatives.

While oil based fuel was not available, the hemp seed oil gave this group options. After much discussion, the survivors of the plague developed a plan to form a caravan and move west toward a safer environment. It took two years to assemble the caravan, and another year to reach Grand Junction. Each of the 40 foot trailers held two families and all their possessions necessary to start a new life in the west.

Their experience passing through the Denver area was not pleasant. Although most of the city was in ruins, they encountered two different gangs that only retreated after being decimated by the caravan's gunfire. The passage over the mountains in early spring had also been difficult.

The next day I met the leader of the Caravan, Roger Vincent. His father had been the original leader, but died in the second battle with the Denver gangs. We talked for an hour, and he asked if I wanted to join them, since he saw the gun on my belt and the fact that my bike would be my transport and a good vehicle for scouting ahead of the caravan.

I thought about the potential problems if I offered my fertility counseling services to the childless couples in the caravan and asked Roger about it. He considered it for a minute and said. "I believe you should carefully discuss it with any potential clients before proceeding. Almost half of our families could not have the blessing of a child. Two of our couples have joined into a polyamory relationship, to have children. We need the next generation if our community will survive intact. I welcome you to our community. It will take a vote by our senior members, but I'm sure it will be approved."

He came by my campsite later that day and invited me to supper, where I met his wife Carol, and they became my first caravan clients.

I kept busy that summer working every day helping to keep the systems maintained and operating. We ran a flexible two-inch pipeline a half mile down to the river to supply the camp and the crop irrigation. I also helped connect and support the electrical system which was fed by either solar panels or a diesel generator.

We would go to town every Market Day. I continued my practice of reading and telling stories to the children on Market Day, and it helped to generate good will among the locals. The townspeople were skeptical at first, but the fact that the Caravan was spending silver in the town, and freely showing those interested, how to grow and use hemp seed oil to power diesel engines, quickly overcame any feelings of mistrust.

By the end of August, the crop was in and there was a surplus of hemp oil after the tankers and all the tanks had been filled. The balance of the oil was traded for a GMC diesel pickup that had been in a barn since diesel fuel had become impossible to get. I became the designated scout vehicle driver, even though I had never driven a vehicle before then. After a few minutes instruction I was comfortable driving at the normal caravan speed of 20 miles per hour.

The other harvest for the caravan was 11 babies on the way. I still had a waiting list of clients and had pulled it off making no enemies.

The caravan departed Grand Junction and continued west on US 70/50. There was a good deal of apprehension in the caravan about the reception we would receive from from the Mormon population in Utah We heard from people in Grand Junction about non-believers being forbidden to enter some of the larger towns.

After near hostile receptions in the few tiny communities we passed through, the decision was made to leave US 70 and stay on US 50 to bypass Salt Lake City.

Another factor was the need to find a safe place to stop for the winter. When the snow started it would be too dangerous to stay on the road.

We turned north on US 50 outside of Salina, Utah. At the edge of town was a sign warning non-believers to not enter. I waited for the caravan to catch up, and after a short discussion with the leaders, Roger

Vincent got in beside me carrying an AR15. We approached a group of men standing in the middle of the road.

Roger told me to stay in the truck and walked the last 20 feet to the group. Their sometimes animated discussions took ten minutes. He returned to the truck, climbed into the bed, and motioned for the caravan to follow us. I moved out after they were behind me, and we drove slowly through the town.

After we were though the town, I asked Roger what he told the group of men.

"I told them we meant their community no harm, but we would continue through on 50, with their permission, or without it. When they refused, I told them we were heavily armed, and prepared to leave their town as a corpse filled ruin if anyone attempted to stop us. They were all carrying flintlocks and the sight of the AR on my shoulder made an impression. Their permission to pass was given grudgingly, after they recognized that discretion was the better part of valor."

Three days later we rolled into Delta, Utah. The town looked deserted, except for two farms west of town. We stopped for the evening and made camp. The next morning two men approached on horseback.

Jason Delgado, his son Ramon, and their families had been living and working on the largest dairy farm in the area.

Delgado relayed his story. "Toward the end of the crash, when LA declared bankruptcy, the power plant shut down because the workers weren't being paid. That killed the mine and everything else in the area. When the railroad and the trucks couldn't get fuel, there was no market for milk or hay, and all the farms shut down.

"A lot of the population left that year while they still had fuel to get out. When the plague hit, the hospital was abandoned, and most of the rest just gave up and left. Many said the town was cursed because of the Gunnison massacre in 1853 when a band of Indians killed most of a US government survey party, as a reprisal of the murder of their chief by a white man.

"We stayed here because we had nowhere to go, and I knew that we could grow enough food and stock to eat. Mr. Madison, the owner of the farm, wrote out a deed before he and his family left. He said it would give me a legal claim on the land, and I would deserve it for taking care of the land and the stock. I think he wouldn't have left, except both his kids were sick, and needed a doctor. I told him I would give the deed back to him if he came back."

Within another day, the caravan was settling into their winter quarters. The town, except for places like the Walmart hadn't been stripped or salvaged. The people from the town left, taking what they could carry. Everyone in the caravan found winter homes that were more comfortable than their mobile quarters had been. I moved into an apartment off Main Street. It had a cast-iron stove, and there was plenty of coal available at the power plant.

By the time the snow came, one of the auxiliary diesel generators at the power plant was isolated from the external loads, and the town had electric power from sunup until two hours after sundown. The power also allowed the pumps to refill the town's water tower. I was one of those mechanically inclined, who took regular shifts operating the power plant.

Others took regular shifts out at the Delgado farm, helping to take care of the livestock in their winter shelters.

I continued to service my clients, including a couple of the locals. There was a used bookstore on Main Street, It had been picked over, but I found a three-ring binder full of printed web pages about organic no-till farming. I spent a lot of my free time carefully reading and absorbing the information. Most of the pages had been written by a young couple of family farmers from Northern California. They had a farm called Laughing Frog in Sevastopol, California.

It was soon obvious to everyone that Delta represented the safe destination they were looking for, since starting their journey. The families planned to make Delta their permanent homes. There was plenty of fertile land, water, and the location was remote enough to make intruders unlikely.

I thought a lot about my future, the families I had assisted, and the potential for problems after their children were born. Some of the women had developed strong feelings for me, and I could foresee the potential for conflicts. The possibility for that, was the last thing I wanted to happen. Shortly after the new year, I decided to leave as soon as the roads were passable.

I spoke to Roger Vincent and told him of my decision, and the reasons for it. He listened without comment, and then told me he understood, but I would be missed. I asked him to not make an announcement since I wanted to say a quick goodbye and ride away.

The snow had melted from the roads and it was receding on the mountains when I started packing. There was a lot of stuff I wanted to take, but just couldn't without overloading the bike. I made a list of the useful things I was leaving, to give to Roger.

When I handed the list to him the day before I planned to leave, he replied, "That won't be necessary. Come over to the Fire Station at mid-day."

I was confused, and he wouldn't answer my questions. I spent the rest of the morning visiting my last three clients, who were just showing. I gave them my usual speech about the apple seed, and I got the feeling that something was going on that I didn't know about.

As I approached the Fire Station I could see a large crowd which turned out to be the entire community. As I walked up, the roll-up door opened and Roger was standing there, with his family. Behind him was the GMC pickup. It was polished until it shown, and a camper shell was on the bed.

Roger motioned for the crowd to be quiet and then spoke. "Danny, you have been an important part of this community and have brought joy into the hearts of many families. This community understands your need to continue your journey and want to help you along the way. We have unanimously voted to give you this truck, hoping you will be successful in your continued efforts to help people. It is equipped with a 200 gallon tank filled with diesel, 100 pounds of hemp seed, and a small press. We would like to ask that you share the hemp oil process with those you meet in your journey. I'm sure you will also have room for the list of things you wanted to give away."

I couldn't keep the tears from flowing, or find the words to express my gratitude to the community I had grown to love.

The next morning, I finished packing up and headed west on US 50.

On the Road Again

US 50 WAS IN ROUGH shape with cracked asphalt, washouts and occasionally drifting sand. I camped the first night in much greater comfort than I had enjoyed in my earlier travels on my bike. The tank was fitted to the pickup bed, and a plywood shelf above it held a mattress and all of my supplies.

I reached the town of Ely, Nevada by sundown the next day. Ely was mostly deserted, with only a dozen families still living there. They were surviving by growing small gardens, raising goats and chickens. I was welcomed to have dinner with one family and gave them a handful of hemp seeds and a discussion about the advantages of no till farming. They had three kids, ranging from a ten year old girl to a baby.

Over the next three days I passed through lots of desolate countryside, and a handful of deserted towns. I arrived in Fallon, Nevada at mid-morning and found a small community just hanging on. With the crash of the Federal and State governments, the closing of the Naval Air Station and the largest employer, most residents abandoned the area. I found a total of 27 families living in the area and getting by in small farms. I wanted to gain information about the best way to travel over the mountains to the west.

I found that in the days after the crash, a group of Reno residents formed a militia to keep the California hoards from overrunning their homes. They were well armed, from the area Nevada National Guard armories. They blew up several sections of the US 80 freeway and effectively sealed it off.

Although decimated during the plague, the community retained a strong militia. They kept strangers away from their community and started extracting a tax, or tithe, for protection, from all the surrounding areas. They also had a reputation for confiscating weapons and other useful items from anyone not in their community. The Reno feudal community also was evolving socially. Young women of marriageable age would sexually sample prospective mates. If a pregnancy did not develop, the young man would be discarded. Because fertile men were in short supply, polygamy became the accepted practice by those women who wanted a child.

The infertile young men joined the militia most of the time, and rapes during the tithe collections were common.

The militia would confiscate my truck and most of my stuff if I let myself fall into their clutches. I passed out a few hemp seeds and verbal information on no-till farming in a series of meetings with families there. They all suggested that I avoid the Reno area, in my quest to reach California.

I left Fallon after a warning that a militia tax collection patrol was sighted on the road from US 80. They were on horseback with a couple of wagons, so I left well before I was sighted. I continued heading west on US 50, and passed through a couple of small farming communities without stopping.

Carson City was the capital of Nevada at the time of the crash and the area was relatively intact. The surrounding land contained many small subsistence farms.

I stopped at the ones nearest the highway to inquire about the best way through the mountains into California. The people were surprised to see a running motor vehicle, and I would explain about the hemp oil fuel, and give them a few seeds. When a family invited me to have supper about sundown, I accepted, and spent the night parked in front of their house.

They suggested I could get more information downtown, because the next day was Market Day and most everyone in the community would be there.

The next morning, I found a place on the Market Square to park, and spent the day answering questions about the truck, hemp oil fuel, and asking about the best passage over the mountains to the west.

What I found out was not encouraging. In the closing days of the crash, the Governor of Nevada issued a call for all citizens to mobilize and prevent the mobs of fleeing Californians from entering and pillaging Nevada. That effort was largely successful, with highways blocked, bridges destroyed, and manned roadblocks.

After a couple of years the attempts to travel east into Nevada stopped altogether, and the blockades continued until the plague broke out. The survivors retreated into enclaves where there was enough food and water to survive. I was also dismayed to hear that the Reno Militia made regular visits to Carson City to extract tithes.

By the end of the day, I was discouraged about finding a way west in this area. A young couple approached and asked if I was the guy looking for information about a way to go over the mountains. The young man told me he had been researching that subject for a long time. When I tried to get more information, he said that we needed to talk privately, and asked me to join him and his wife for supper.

I gave them a lift to his family's farm on the south side of town. The Benton Farm looked to be about 20 acres, with a windmill, a barn, and a cluster of small houses around a large home. Tom and Jessie Benton lived in one of the small houses. He was the youngest of three sons, and as such, would not receive a share of the family farm when his father died.

There wasn't any farmland in the area available that had water and his prospects were limited to working as a field hand for one of his brothers, or trying to find work in Reno.

He had resolved to find a way over the mountains to seek his fortune and a better life in California, which had more water available. His plans were altered when he fell in love and married Jessie. While Jessie cooked dinner over a wood stove Tom poured me a mug of beer and appeared ready to talk.

Tom sighed and said, "The militia set up artillery in south Lake Tahoe and blocked the highway by blowing up a line of vehicles attempting to come down the hill. A year ago I climbed the hill and there is a line of abandoned vehicles blocking the roadway, extending as far as I could see. They were packed in so tight that no one could turn around, although many crashed attempting to.

"I heard stories that the road is blocked by abandoned vehicles all the way back to near Sacramento. I heard that when the grid went down, the cartels swept up from Mexico and started plundering everything. The people panicked, and the mob fled north seeking shelter and safety.

"Last fall, I believe I found a way over the mountains. It will take clearing debris from a landslide, but other than a lot of work, I don't think it is impassable."

I replied, "Exactly where is it located?"

"We'll get to the details after supper, I can see Jessie has the look, I better not ignore."

The couple were my age and appeared to be a good match. Jessie was an excellent cook, and I could see that they loved each other deeply.

After the meal, I opened a bottle of hard apple cider and poured my hosts a drink.

I opened the conversation by asking what they wanted for the yet undisclosed information.

Tom laughed, and answered, "Yes, there is a price for information. We would like you to give us a ride over the mountain to a place that looks like a safe location to settle and make a new life. We must work together to clear the road at the landslide, and there may be dangers to face, so we will be safer traveling together. I have a couple of guns with some ammunition. We also have some farming equipment we can strap to the rack on top of your truck."

I knew that I needed to get across the mountains before the winter, and that the longer I took trying to find a way, the more likely I would be to run into the militia.

"You drive a hard bargain, but I have one condition."

"What's that?" Tom inquired.

"Jessie has to do the cooking while we're together."

She smiled, and said, "I'll be happy to do that."

We had breakfast at the big house where I met Tom's father, Howard. He was a big boisterous man, who seemed relieved that his youngest son was not going to be a burden to his brothers. The increased tithes were making it difficult to support everyone with what the farm could produce.

I also met Tom's younger sister, Callie. She was short, outspoken, looked about 15, with flaming red hair, green eyes, and was developing into a beautiful young woman.

We spent the day loading the truck, and I was glad the load wasn't too heavy. It was bulky, and included hand tools, a push plow, and cages that contained chickens and four piglets. It was packed, and probably a little top heavy, but everything they wanted to take was loaded.

Supper was at the big house with all the family, including the older brothers and their families. As I was walking out, Howard put his arm over my shoulder and said how much he appreciated me helping his son chase his dream. He also slipped two twenty dollar gold eagles into my pocket.

We left early the next morning, headed south on Highway 88, and crossed into California by late morning. We started climbing toward Carson Pass and reached the blocked area just before dark. I stopped on a level spot and walked toward the landslide covering the road. Tom and Jessie started unpacking their tent.

I had decided that it was getting too dark to climb around the boulders blocking the road and turned back toward the truck.

At that point, Tom shouted, "Danny, we have a little problem."

I ran toward the truck when Tom stepped out from behind it. He was accompanied by a smaller figure.

"We have a stow-away. I'm really sorry about this. She begged us to come along, but I refused to consider it."

I got a closer look and realized that our stow-away was Tom's sister, Callie.

She pulled away from Tom's grasp and ran to meet me. "Oh please Mr. Martin, I had to go. I won't be any trouble, and I can't stand the thought of being militia bait. I'll do anything, even be your bed warmer. Just don't send me back."

I frowned, and said. "I'm not a pedophile, and I don't want or need a bed warmer. I won't leave a kid out here, and I don't want to waste the time to take you back. I guess I'm stuck with you.

"Tom, you and Jessie will have to look out for her, and make sure she pulls her weight.

"Callie, did you bring a bedroll and a tent?"

"No, no sir, I just made up my mind to do it at the last minute. I'm sorry."

Tom responded, "She can sleep in the tent with us."

I answered, "You two need a little privacy. She can use the spare blankets and the other side of the mattress. I don't require a Queen size bed.

"Now Callie, get busy gathering some firewood. Tomorrow's gonna be a long day."

The next 30 days were long and hard. With two shovels, a pick, a crow bar, and the bike trailer we moved tons of rock and debris to clear a narrow path on the outer edge of the road.

On July 28th, we were finally able to squeeze the truck through. It was late afternoon, and we all agreed to stop for the night at Caples

Lake , only 3 miles west. We turned off Highway 88 at the entrance to the Caples Lake Resort. It was abandoned, and we parked at the water's edge. The temperature had been in the low 80's and we were all more than a little ripe.

Jessie took off her clothes and announced, "I don't know about you guys, but I'm getting naked, and washing myself and my clothes."

I hesitated, since I was not family, and Jessie called out, "Don't be bashful Danny, we aren't."

The water was ice cold and quickly eliminated any concern that the sight of two delightful naked females might cause me to become aroused. It was invigorating, and while our clothes started to dry, Tom and Jessie retired to their tent, and Callie and I to our bedrolls.

Callie spoke, with an innocent look on her face. "I read somewhere that we'll get warm quicker by cuddling up. I'm willing to try it. Are you?"

I grinned at her and answered. "Your offer sounds like fun, but I'm sure that something would come up, and I don't shoot blanks."

She looked disappointed, and a little confused and said. "At least put your arm around me and cuddle me through the blankets."

An hour later, she hopped out of her blankets and retrieved our mostly dry clothes. She was careful to show me as she dressed, everything I had missed getting close to. I waited until she moved out of sight before I got dressed. Cold, damp jeans were also capable of cooling my ardor.

The next morning we continued west and found a car stopped in the middle of the road. It didn't look like it had been stripped and I stopped for a closer inspection. As soon as I saw the skeletons in the front seat, I flashed back to the SUV I found back in New Mexico. Again, both people in the front seat had shattered skulls, and so did the child in the woman's arms.

They must have run out of fuel after not being able to get past the landslide. I couldn't imagine the desperation that had driven a man to kill his family and himself. We didn't attempt to salvage anything in the car, and there was little conversation for the rest of the day.

We camped at the junction of Highway 88 and a road leading to Plymouth, California. My planned destination was Sonoma County, which I had read about in the stories on No-Till farming. Going through Plymouth was the most direct way there. Tom and Jessie had been non committal about where they wanted to go, and readily agreed to see what Sonoma County had to offer.

We found that Plymouth was in ruins, with many shot up and burned buildings and vehicles. We did find three families living in an intact house and farming a couple of garden plots. The people were fearful, but warmed up when we presented no threat. They were survivors, who had fled into the mountains both times the mobs came through. There had been no strangers through since the plague.

There were a couple of young men there who attempted to catch Callie's eye, but she was not interested.

We gave them some seeds and headed north on Highway 49 the next day. They couldn't tell us much about the Sacramento area, except that the city had mostly burned.

We passed through a few small communities that were in the same state of ruin as Plymouth until we reached US 50. The Eastbound lanes were filled with abandoned cars. Many were shot up or burned. The Westbound lanes had a few cars, but were passable. As we continued west, the view from the freeway was depressing. There was no signs of life and the communities looked like a war zone.

We stopped for the night near the junction of I 5, which was blocked in both directions as far as I could see. Our camp was on the freeway so we had good visibility in all directions. There was still no signs of life, but plenty of evidence of violence and desperation in all directions.

The next morning we turned around and took the first off ramp into downtown Sacramento. We spent the day wondering around the city, working around various obstructions toward the Northwest. Just before sundown we crossed the river and made camp ten miles north of where we camped the previous night.

The next day we crossed the I 5 again and turned west toward Woodland.

We saw a few farms off in the distance, but nothing close to the roads we were on. Over the next three days we wondered through Yolo County, heading west and south. We passed south of Lake Berryessa and turned to the Northwest on 128. As we passed through the many vineyards and small farms a distinct pattern was apparent. They were all abandoned, and many were burned.

We followed 128 north to the town of St. Helena. There we found a community of around a hundred people who lived in town and worked in the surrounding farms and vineyards. They were wary of strangers, but willing to talk about their lives and experience during the crash. Most of the older ones fled into the mountains on either side of the town and hid out until the mob had passed through to the north. They returned to find their homes and farms plundered of anything edible and stripped or burned.

No one we talked to had any direct experience with Sonoma County, and most expected it was as hard pressed as St. Helena.

I decided to go to the north of Santa Rosa, which had been a city of over 150,000 before the crash. We left St. Helena early in the morning and rolled into Sebastopol in the late afternoon.

My first impression was that the rolling tree-covered hills felt like home. I saw several cultivated fields near the town. People were walking from them into the town. They were very interested in our vehicle. By the time we stopped on Main Street, there was a crowd of 30 people gathered around us.

I asked the crowd if anyone could direct us to the Laughing Frog Farm. An old man pointed toward west and said it had been burned in the crash and was abandoned, about three miles out Bodega Highway on the right.

I thanked him, returned to the cab and started driving away. Callie spotted the faded sign, and we turned into a dirt path. The light was fading when I stopped in front of the ruins of what had been a large home. We camped in front of it and would wait for morning to explore our new home.

Home At Last

THE NEXT MORNING, WE surveyed the property. Beside the ruins of a large two story home there were two steel buildings, a row of four re-purposed shipping containers. One was configured as a kitchen and dining hall, and the other three, as tiny homes. There was also a chicken coop, and an animal pen which we quickly put to use for our birds and piglets. Inside one barn was a Kubota tractor. Its fuel line had been cut and the diesel drained. The rear tires were flat, but it looked like it could be restored to operation.

The kitchen range used propane, and there was a large buried tank behind the barn. The gage on the tank showed it was still half full. At the end of the shop building was an ancient Lister diesel generator. The fuel tank that fed it was empty, but I figured we could get it running sooner or later.

Tom and Jessie already moved their things into one of the tiny houses, and Callie was looking at me with a question in her eyes. I knew it was time to make some disclosures, and a decision. I dug my backpack out of the truck and asked the others to join me in the kitchen.

"It's time to get a few things established. It should clear the air and help us in planning our future. I haven't disclosed what I consider as my calling."

I tossed my business card on the Table where the three of them were sitting. It read:

Danny Appleseed
Tinker, Teacher,

and

Baby Maker

"Since I started my journey, I have helped at least 41 infertile families start a wanted child by impregnating the mothers. I plan to continue providing those services as long as I can.

"If you, Tom and Jessie, want my help, I'll do my best. If you believe that it would be best for you to not live here with me, I understand."

Callie sat there with an anguished look on her face. "You said that you don't shoot blanks, and now I understand."

"Yes Callie, I am very attracted to you and would love to make you my life partner. But, you will have to understand that I'm committed to helping families have the children they desperately want and need."

Tears streamed down her face and she said. "I must think about this, and talk with my brother. It's so new, I don't know what to think about it."

"I'll spend the afternoon walking the property. We'll talk more before supper."

When I completed my property survey, I took my things from the truck and put them in the tiny house furthest away from Tom and Jessie. After a nap, I returned to the kitchen and found the three of them waiting.

Tom opened the conversation. "Jessie and I know the man you are, and we will be proud to have you give what I cannot. I have grown to love you like a brother, and we want to stay right here and build a life for us and our children at Laughing Frog Farm."

Callie looked mysterious, and said. "Your offer isn't anything I imagined my Prince Charming would ever say. Sharing you with an untold number of other women, even my sister-in-law, is beyond my comprehension. But, I think I know where you are coming from. Our world has changed, and the only way for our children to have even a bare chance at normal lives, is to do everything possible to build strong families. Children will do that.

"I also know now that love isn't a limited commodity. I believe that when you give your love to others, It will not limit the love you have for me and our children. And yes, we will have lots of them, so you better not have any blanks for me.

"Now, it's time for you to do what I've wanted since that day at Caples Lake."

She launched herself into my arms, and I carried her into our tiny home. I had no reply, since words weren't important. We made love into the night, and again in the morning.

Two days later, I spent the afternoon with Jessie, in her bed in our first try at starting a baby for her family.

Over the next month we planted a fall garden and a half acre of hemp. We got to know our neighbors, and I spent Market Days tinkering, teaching, and offering fertility services. By the end of the first month I had two new clients. By the time to harvest the hemp we had both the generator and the tractor running. We pressed enough hemp oil to run the generator all winter. I was spending two nights a week servicing clients and both Callie and Jessie were pregnant.

The winter was cold, wet, and dreary. We spent it working inside on a range of projects. Surplus hemp seeds were traded for the grain and corn we would use over the winter, and we pressed hemp seed oil for three neighbors in exchange for various items.

With the spring, we planted nine acres in a variety of crops. The topsoil was thick and rich, largely from the prior owner's no till planting procedures. The baby making process now included seven on the way, and three more in work.

Once a month, we would load the truck and go to Santa Rosa for Market Day. The city had been devastated by the mobs coming out of the Bay Area. The population was only a tenth of what it had been in the pre-crash days. On one July Market Day I found several pages in a notebook written by a Mr. Patrick Humphrey, an author and a History Teacher, which described the crash in California.

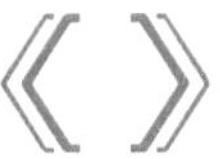

The Late Great State of California

THE CRASH RESULTED from too many years of governments, corporations, and Banks kicking the can down the road. Combinations of debt, derivatives, and corruption became unsustainable.

The trigger point was the immigrant riots in Europe. Burning cities pushed countries already on the brink into economic collapse. Derivatives failed, slowly at first and then faster and faster. Firewalls and other emergency measures to contain the developing disaster were erected and failed. The interconnected world economy fractured and died.

The effects of the crash cascaded down as bankrupt governments printed more paper money and inflation roared. Companies made massive cutbacks. Even government employees encountered bounced and missing paychecks.

Unpaid utility workers stopped going to work, and power plants ceased operations. Stores closed and just in time deliveries of food, fuel, and other necessities became unavailable. Emergency police, fire, and medical service disappeared.

In California, the vacuum caused by the loss of police and National Guard law enforcement was filled by the cartel gangs. Sweeping up from Mexico, they joined their compatriots in Southern California to plunder a defenseless population.

The panic was all-consuming, and the population attempted to escape the metropolitan areas. Within days, freeways were gridlocked, with people leaving their trapped vehicles and attempting to walk to safety. The gangs followed, leaving a trail of plunder, rape, murder, and devastation. They either bypassed any pockets of resistance or burned them out.

The mobs with fuel remaining poured north and east from Southern California. Those who traveled east met the Nevada Militia, who blocked their entry with automatic weapons. Within a week, the interstate and the desert were filled with the dead and soon to be.

The mobs heading north pushed through the central valley and along the coast. They encountered mobs fleeing the bay area and more gangs.

Within a month, the cities of Southern California became a burnt out war zone, with enclaves controlled by different gangs. The gangs had lots of plunder and willing slaves initially. But, soon the supplies of plundered food and fuel became short. Warfare, between the gangs over the shrinking supplies became the rule, rather than the exception.

In Northern California, the mobs leaving the bay area ran into the same merciless blockades when they attempted to enter Nevada on US 50 or US 80. The gangs rampaged throughout the region with the same results that occurred in Southern California.

During the first winter after the crash, starvation stalked the state. The central valley, once "Breadbasket of America" lay fallow, and the warehouses holding food were plundered. Even those individuals who planned to live off the land, quickly found there were more hunters and gathers than game or edible plants.

The plague hit that summer and killed off half of the surviving population. By the next year a large percentage of the surviving men were infertile.

As the gangs depleted their fuel and food they starved in their enclaves. Some even resorted to cannibalizum.

As far as I know, Southern California is now a barren, lifeless, wasteland.

In isolated pockets where it was possible, a few survivors grew gardens, and many survived the following winter.

With good fortune, some of us will learn how to survive and prosper in this new and different world. Our lives will be subsistence based for many years. I hope we will retain the knowledge base from before the crash, and I hope we will develop the wisdom to avoid the actions that led to it.

Epilogue

IT HAS BEEN 60 YEARS since I left my home in New Mexico, and a lot of water has run under the bridge. Callie passed last month surrounded by those who loved her. I expect to follow her soon.

Our population is no longer trapped in isolated pockets, surviving by meager subsistence farming, and the effects of the plague infertility are not present in my children's generation.

While our world has changed drastically, we have started to rebuild. Travel and industry are still limited, but radio communications have allowed our scattered communities to re-establish contacts.

My oldest son found some ham radio equipment at a Santa Rosa Market Day when he was 14. When he started listening to occasional short-wave broadcasts, it became his life's calling.

Within a year, he was regularly communicating with communities all over the west. By the time he was 16 he had restored an AM broadcast station, which became a must listen to feature in the area.

Hemp oil production is widespread, with each community growing enough to supply their own needs. The diesel engines and vehicles are all salvaged, and the only new items are replacement parts.

Electric power production is primarily by salvaged diesel generators, with limited hydro, wind, and solar using salvaged components. There is no grid connections, only local plants where the users sharing to provide the operating and maintenance labor, and fuel.

No-till farming is the rule, rather than the exception although it has proven to be more labor intensive. Powered machines are still limited, even with the ability to fuel them with hemp oil.

I have been able to keep in touch with friends in the Delta, Red River, and Taos communities with help from my radio expert son. All three communities have survived and prospered.

I had a report from Roswell that my uncle was killed by his own son, Jerry, who was later convicted of murder and hung.

Laughing Frog Farm now has a large apple orchard as its primary crop. We still produce enough hemp oil to meet our fuel needs, and most of our food.

The farmhouse was rebuilt, even larger, and it presently houses the four multi-generation families that run the farm. I still live in one of the tiny houses, and the other three were configured as a large nursery and school for the younger kids.

My tinkering and baby making days are long past, and I spend most of my days sitting in my rocking chair reading and telling stories to the younger children.

Author Notes

THANKS FOR READING this book. I would appreciate your review where you purchased it, and any feedback or comments you may have. If you are interested in becoming a beta reader of my prerelease books, please contact me at:

agkatfri@mail.com

You can visit my web site at:

https://www.agkbooksandblog.com[1]

I'm a writer, and I write about what interests me, stories that I would enjoy reading. As an insatiable reader since grade school, and frequently in trouble for reading in class, I soon discovered science fiction. When I read Heinlein's Stranger in a strange land, I Grokked, and the die was cast.

Many of my books are hard science fiction and don't include steam punk, fantasy, magic, elves or faeries.

As a naval and military history buff, I also have written several books that feature warships, aircraft, airships, spacecraft, and military action.

A recovering engineer, I discovered the internet early. I spend a few hours each morning keeping a finger on current events, technologies, human relations, and the body politic. I became interested in Prepping during the Y2K period, and follow the survival industry, and alternate energy technologies. Using that background, I have written several dystopian books.

---

1. https://www.agkbooksandblog.com/

Several of my books contain adult situations and content, because real adults, when thrown together by stressful events, will have adult relationships. I show some of my characters experiencing them.

I have a wide range of life experiences that contribute to my knowledge base and interests. They include: I dug ditches for a plumber, and loaded bread trucks in High School. The Navy educated me in electronics and I worked on radar systems. Afterward, I continued working in electronics for the defense industry, just as the Navy was transitioning to digital computers. That experience led me into a 30+ year career in the welding automation industry as an engineer, exec, and CEO.

A mild heart attack shifted my priorities, and I spent the next several years running a charter boat in North Carolina. I would take families out and teach the kids how to fish, while telling them stories about the pirates and blockade runners who were in the area.

I published my first book, BB-39 in 2012 after finally retiring for the fourth time. I still produce two or three books a year. My eyes and knees are shot. But any day I can get vertical is a good day.

If "Things get better with age" then this 1944 model is approaching excellent.

All of my Book Links are at:
https://books2read.com/ap/8Zj2D8/AG-Kimbrough

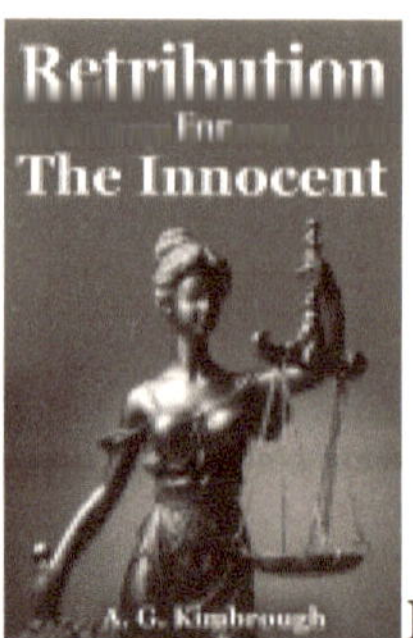**Retribution for The Innocent**

Scott Clark reinvented himself after losing a leg in the sandbox. He successfully applied his computer skills as a Cybernetic Private Investigator.

An investigation into a high-level criminal coverup reveals an untouchable pedophile. Subsequently, Clark uncovers a vast network of untouchable pedophiles, their suppliers, and supporters. With no justice available from the Justice System, Clark and the Saxon Justice Committee have declared war on them.

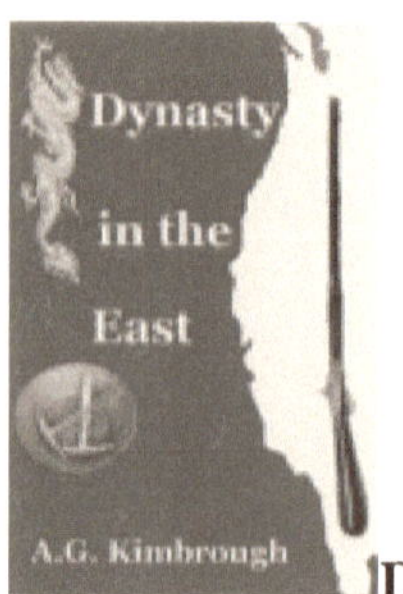**Dynasty in the East** - *Released in 2022*

This Alternate History Saga begins in 1405, when a late departing element of the First Chinese Treasure Fleet is driven far to the north by a major typhoon. They sail due east in an attempt to catch up with the rest of the fleet, and make landfall in the Americas. After trading for a hoard of

Inca gold, they sail north and establish a colony in northern California.

MERIWETHER LEWIS BUYS a Girandoni repeating air rifle with his own money at the Brown's Ferry Arsenal, while purchasing guns and supplies for the Corps of Discovery Expedition.

That rifle has a profound effect in the Empire, the Alamo, and in the Civil War.

Historical figures, including: William Clark, Davy Crockett, Quincy Adams, Danial Webster, Andy Jackson, Robert E. Lee, Abraham Lincoln and others who will play rolls in this saga which continues into the 1880's.

BB-39

This Greatest Generation Novel chronicles the story of five young men stationed on the USS Arizona in the prewar US Navy and beyond. Events fracture their friendships, loves, and lives. Forged by a conflict greater than themselves, they move in divergent paths. Until 1990, an accident starts another chain of events that brings redemption, twilight lovers reunited, and a Siberian POW rescued.

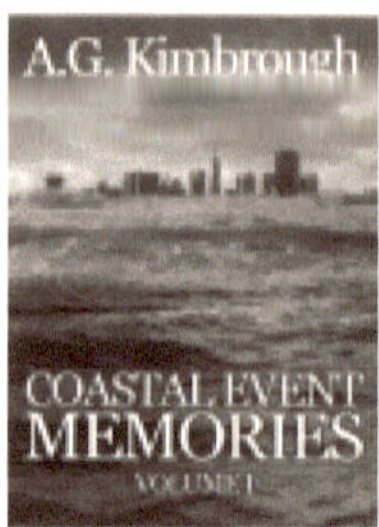**Coastal Event Memories Volume 1**

This is the first of five Novellas in a near term Science Fiction Post-Apocalyptic series. Each book in the series tells the stories of a group of survivors that live through a Global Extermination Event. The characters in this book are clustered around the shores of a great Inland Sea above what used to be called the San Joaquin Valley in California. These stories were triggered by current events shortly after I published my first book, BB-39. I had planned to complete another long-delayed novel, but these stories could not be set aside. Finally, I gave up and started writing these stories about people living in a world with vast areas covered by many feet of volcanic ash, and where the sea levels have risen by over 300 feet.

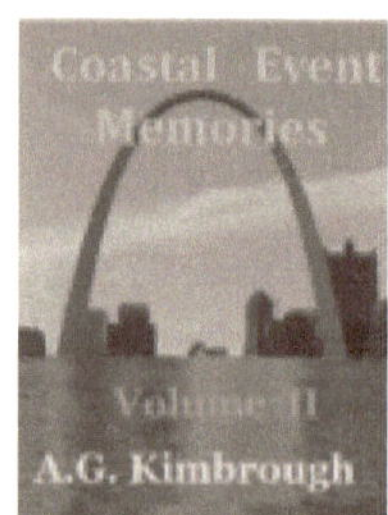**Coastal Event Memories Volume 2**

This is the second in a series of near-term Science Fiction Post-apocalyptic Novellas. It tells the stories of another group of survivors who live through the same species-ending series of global catastrophes described in Volume 1.

North America is slammed by a series of massive earthquakes and volcanic eruptions, followed by super-hurricane force winds and months of driving rain. The coastal regions are swallowed by a 300-foot sea level rise.

The primary location for this story is the Smokey Mountains of the western Carolinas.

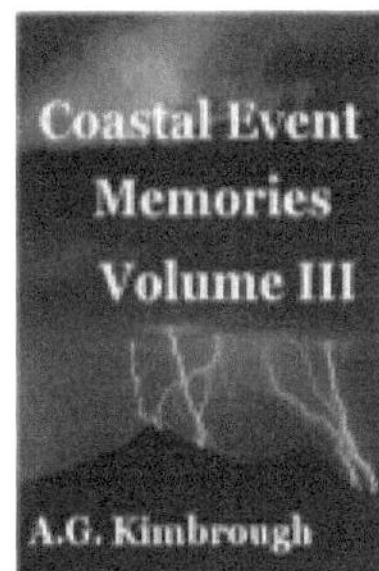Coastal Event Memories Volume 3

This Science Fiction Post-apocalyptic Novella is the third in a series that tell the stories of a small group of normal people thrust into a Global Extinction Event. Fate, tenacity, and a will to live help these individuals survive where millions have perished.

This group of strangers, thrown together by the Event, finds unconventional relationships. They form a band to make a desperate run for home across the southwest, threading a needle between volcanic lava and ash to the north, and barbarous gangs of cartel murderers laying waste to survivors in the southwest.

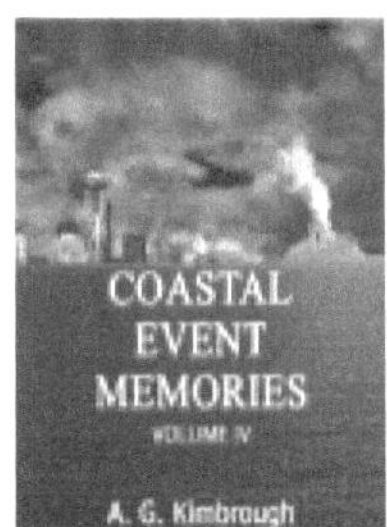Coastal Event Memories Volume 4

In galactic terms, the Earth lives in a dangerous neighborhood. Seven times in the past humanity has reached for the stars, only to have their civilization destroyed by an extinction event. The scattered surviving pockets of humanity returned to a meager agrarian existence, with little or no retention of their prior technology and knowledge base. As fuel and food stocks were depleted, those survivors without the ability to acquire more, perished.

This Novella tells the stories of a small band of a present-day extinction event survivors in the Puget Sound area of Washington state. They came through the event due to a combination of fate, tenacity, and a will to live that helped these individuals survive where millions have perished. Their world has changed forever, and they must face the challenges of just surviving, while attempting to retain at least a small part of the technology and civilization which had been reaching for the stars.

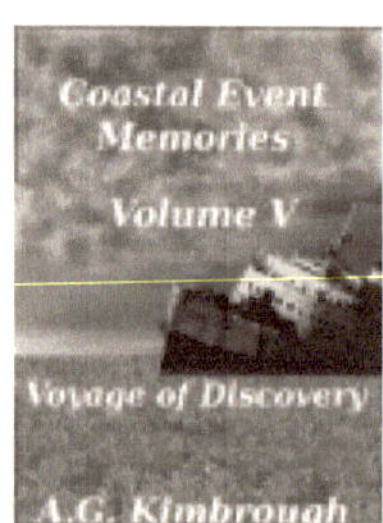

Coastal Event Memories Volume 5

This Novella tells the story, set 60 years after the Coastal Event, of the start of a voyage of discovery by the descendants of the event survivors. They embark on an around-the-world sea voyage to seek out other pockets of humanity. Their objective, is to establish trade and consolidate the knowledge base that humanity has retained. Their forefathers came through the event due to a combination of fate, tenacity, and a will to live that helped these individuals survive where millions have perished.

The world changed forever, before they were born, and while survival is no longer an issue, the challenge of retaining at least a small part of the technology and civilization which had been reaching for the stars is a reality they are now dealing with.

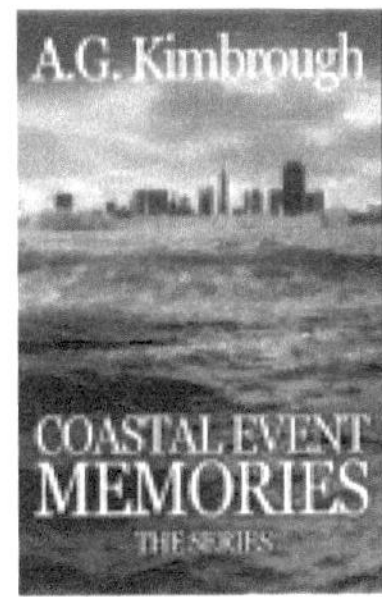**Coastal Event Memories, the Series: Volumes 1 – 5**

These Post-Apocalyptic novellas tell the stories of people who survive a global extermination event with global volcanic eruptions and a 300' sea level rise. These novellas are available as single eBooks, and as a collection in print and eBook formats.

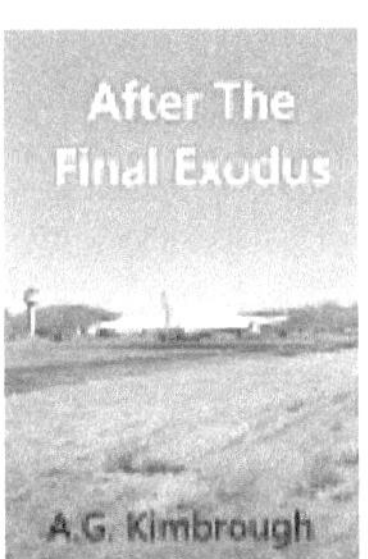

After The Final Exodus

After the Final Exodus is a Science Fiction Novella that is a sequel to the Coastal Event Memories Series. Four-hundred years later, the Coastal Event's survivor descendants have managed to recover much of the pre-event technologies and humanity. After the discovery of proof of a Martin City ruins, the three dominate corporate organizations unite in a crash effort to send a manned ship to the Red Planet.

THE SUCCESSFUL FLIGHT of Enterprise to Mars is completed with a smooth landing near the Martin City ruins. The crew soon discovers that sabotage to their ship has stranded them with no possibility for a safe return. As they contemplated their own mortality, a message from a Phobos based AI welcomes them to the Federation of Sentient Space-faring Races. Later, the crew learns of a looming Extermination Event that will doom the entire population of the Earth, in less than seventy years.

The AI offers them a means to return home, with a way for Earth's population to escape the final extermination event. All that must be done in the next seventy years, is to construct a fleet of star ships capable of transporting a million people and everything needed for them to build new lives, to a solar system twenty-seven Light Years away.

After The Virus Apocalypse

This story is fiction today, but...

What if a bio-weapon escapes after mutating and the cure no longer works. Suppose it goes dormant after infecting the initial victims. If the victim recovers, the virus returns, without symptoms, to be contagious again before killing the weakened host.

Pandemic Passions

SUMMER FLINGS BETWEEN a pair of entitled New York debutantes and a pair of unlikely best friends, a wealthy geek, and a working class ranch hand, become real, when their world crashes in a global pandemic. This apocalyptic novel may be considered romantic soft porn by some. But, it could be torn from tomorrows headlines.

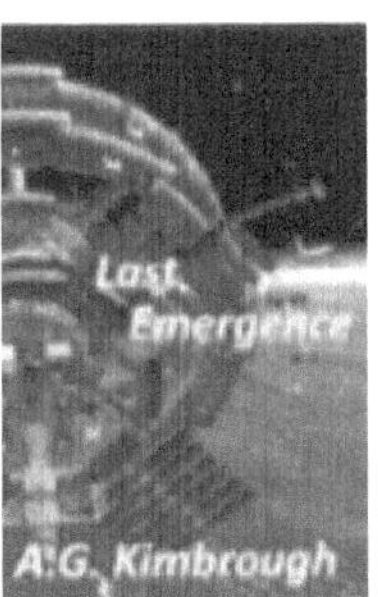

Last Emergence

WHEN MEN FINALLY EMERGED from the bunkers, they had to start rebuilding civilization. Other men watched from orbit, knowing that when radio waves return, so will the aliens, and their Extermination Event weapon.

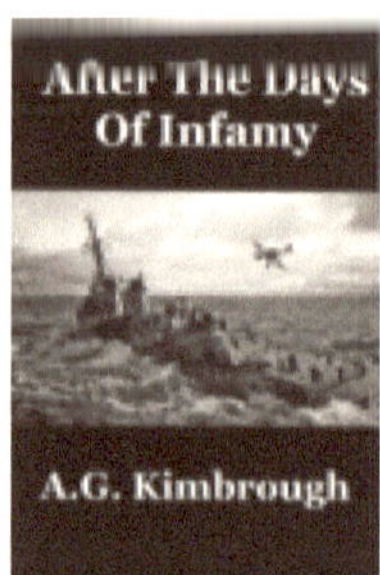

After The Days of Infamy - Book 1

In the first novel of this alternate history trilogy, Japan uses a fleet of Airship Aircraft Carriers to attack Pearl Harbor. Later that same week, the same fleet attacks targets along the United States West Coast.

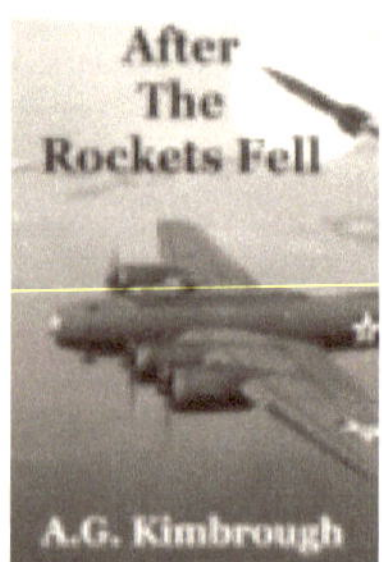

After The Rockets Fell - Book 2

IN THE SECOND NOVEL of this alternate history trilogy, Russia is in full retreat, England is defeated, the Eight Air Force is shattered, Germany controls Europe, and is building a fleet of subs to hit the US with Nerve Gas rockets.

**After Contact - Book 3**

IN THE FINAL NOVEL of this alternate history trilogy, Hitler is dead, the war is over, but, large numbers of German U Boats, key scientists, and engineers, are missing. When rumors of a secret Nazi base developing Super Weapons in the South Atlantic are uncovered, two veteran intelligence agents are sent to Argentina to investigate.

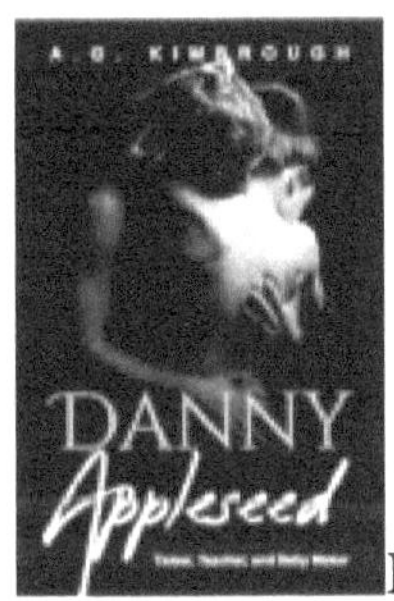Danny Appleseed, Tinker, Teacher, and
Baby Maker

DANNY MARTIN WAS CONCEIVED a month before the second plague wave. His mother survived it, and his DNA was not damaged. Danny is among the 10% of male population who are fertile. At 18, he is on the run from a false murder charge by an Uncle who wants him dead. Danny takes refuge in Taos, New Mexico, 250 miles north of his Uncle's ranch.

Danny found his true calling when approached by a pair of openly lesbian sisters, who are desperate to have a child. They offer to become temporary sex partners with him in the hope that one of them will become pregnant. They are both delighted to find that Danny doesn't shoot blanks. By the end of summer, word spreads in the community, and Danny has helped several client couples start a child.

A narrow escape from a pair of hard-case bounty-hunters forces Danny to leave Taos to avoid endangering his friends and clients. He embarks on a journey that will take him to new places, new couples to help, and a new life.

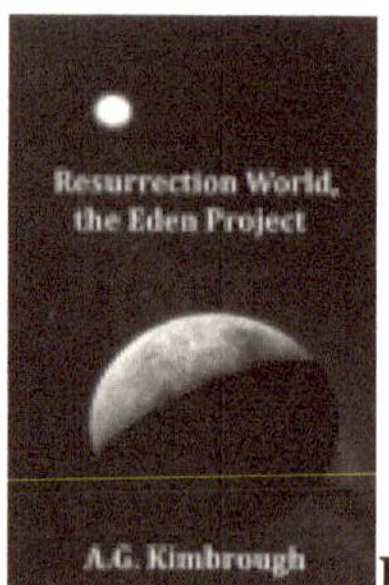**Resurrection World, the Eden Project**

TO SAVE THE HUMAN RACE, the Federation of Space-Faring Sentient Races embarks on a project to resurrect dying humans from 1650, 1864, and 1941, on a terraformed planet far away from Earth.

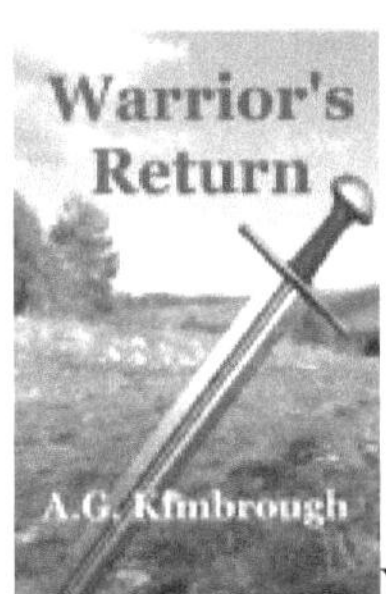

Warrior's Return

Warrior's Return is a novella based on the recovery of Lucid Dreams that provide links to events in the past. AI technology has enabled Mike Tolliver to see a glimpse into events as far back as 32AD. But has it also opened Pandora's Box?

The Days after The Music Died

AFTER A SERIES OF GLOBAL EMP Events, a widely scattered family attempts to escape the madness that is burning the cities and reach a refuge they established on a Mississippi River island.

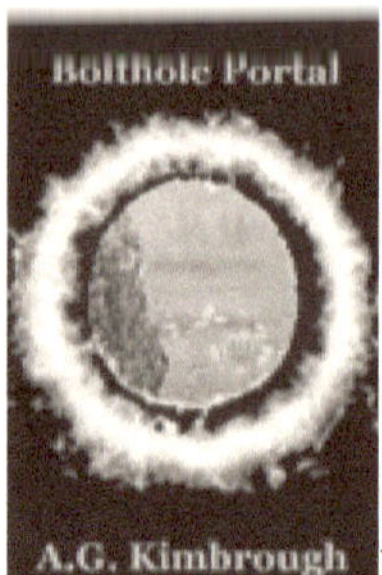**Bolthole Portal**

Cynthia feels the pressure, as every day reduces the time available to save a small sample of humanity.

This time, Nibru will bring an Extinction Event, in less than five years.

A breakthrough physics discovery offers a glimpse of an unknown world beyond a portal. She is directing a project that dwarfs the Manhattan Project, in scope and secrecy.

The United States will attempt to launch, through an expanded portal, a group of its best and brightest young people into the unknown world.

Will the clock reach midnight before Project Bolthole can be completed?

**Renaissance and Reboot in Flyover Country**

An alternate history novel depicting events leading up to the second American Revolution.

After COVID nearly kills him, Jack Harper cashes out of his frantic life in Silicon Valley, and embarks on a quest for a simpler life. An unexpected event lands him in a small northwest Nebraska town for a long weekend.

As Jack searches for information for his blog article about small towns dying in the heartland he learned that he may be part of the problem.

His plan to launch a business incubator is moving ahead until a state-wide COVID lock-down brings progress to a halt. Will Jack have enough cash to complete the project? Can the town be saved?